Books by Shirleen Davies

Historical Western Romance Series
Redemption Mountain

Redemption's Edge, Book One
Wildfire Creek, Book Two
Sunrise Ridge, Book Three
Dixie Moon, Book Four
Survivor Pass, Book Five
Promise Trail, Book Six
Deep River, Book Seven
Courage Canyon, Book Eight
Forsaken Falls, Book Nine
Solitude Gorge, Book Ten
Rogue Rapids, Book Eleven
Angel Peak, Book Twelve
Restless Wind, Book Thirteen
Storm Summit, Book Fourteen
Mystery Mesa, Book Fifteen
Thunder Valley, Book Sixteen
A Very Splendor Christmas, Holiday Novella, Book Seventeen
Paradise Point, Book Eighteen, Coming Next in the Series!

MacLarens of Boundary Mountain

Colin's Quest, Book One,
Brodie's Gamble, Book Two
Quinn's Honor, Book Three

Sam's Legacy, Book Four
Heather's Choice, Book Five
Nate's Destiny, Book Six
Blaine's Wager, Book Seven
Fletcher's Pride, Book Eight
Bay's Desire, Book Nine
Cam's Hope, Book Ten

MacLarens of Fire Mountain

Tougher than the Rest, Book One
Faster than the Rest, Book Two
Harder than the Rest, Book Three
Stronger than the Rest, Book Four
Deadlier than the Rest, Book Five
Wilder than the Rest, Book Six

Romantic Suspense

Eternal Brethren, Military Romantic Suspense

Steadfast, Book One
Shattered, Book Two
Haunted, Book Three
Untamed, Book Four
Devoted, Book Five
Faithful, Book Six
Exposed, Book Seven
Undaunted, Book Eight
Resolute, Book Nine

Unspoken, Book Ten, Coming Next in the Series!

Peregrine Bay, Romantic Suspense

Reclaiming Love, Book One
Our Kind of Love, Book Two
Edge of Love, Book Three, Coming Next in the Series!

Contemporary Romance Series

MacLarens of Fire Mountain

Second Summer, Book One
Hard Landing, Book Two
One More Day, Book Three
All Your Nights, Book Four
Always Love You, Book Five
Hearts Don't Lie, Book Six
No Getting Over You, Book Seven
'Til the Sun Comes Up, Book Eight
Foolish Heart, Book Nine

Macklin's of Burnt River

Thorn's Journey
Del's Choice
Boone's Surrender

The best way to stay in touch is to subscribe to my newsletter. Go to https://www.shirleendavies.com/ and subscribe in the box at the top of the right column that asks for your email.

You'll be notified of new books before they are released, have chances to win great prizes, and receive other subscriber-only specials.

A Very Splendor Christmas

Redemption Mountain
Historical Western Romance Series

SHIRLEEN DAVIES

Book Seventeen in the Redemption Mountain
Historical Western Romance Series

For permission requests, contact the publisher.

Avalanche Ranch Press, LLC
PO Box 12618
Prescott, AZ 86304

A Very Splendor Christmas is a work of fiction. Names, characters, places, and incidents are either products of the author's imagination or used fictitiously. Any resemblance to actual events, locales, or persons, living or dead, is wholly coincidental.

Book design and conversions by Joseph Murray at 3rdplanetpublishing.com

Cover design by Jaycee DeLorenzo at Sweet 'N Spicy Designs

ISBN: 978-1-947680-34-0

I care about quality, so if you find an error, please contact me via email at <u>shirleen@shirleendavies.com</u>

Description

Will the magic of the season bring love to a jaded lawman and cautious woman who doesn't believe in second chances?

A Very Splendor Christmas, Book Seventeen, A Novella, Redemption Mountain Historical Western Romance Series

Hawkins DeBell has been through hell, and lived to start a new life. Leaving his bounty hunting days behind to become a deputy in Splendor, he allowed time to heal from the pain of his past. With no plans to remarry, Hawke enjoys a quiet life, the comradery with fellow deputies, and occasional excitement from his work. Until the day a stunning blonde catches his attention.

Nellie "Beauty" Crawford has survived more than one attempt on her life. With money in the bank, a job, and house near her best friend, Francesca, she wants for nothing. Except perhaps the company of a surly lawman with a painful past.

Christmas is always a joyous time in the frontier town. Families make the long ride from their ranches and farms. Laden with food, those attending Christmas Eve service also look forward to the marriage of Zeke Boudreaux and

Frannie O'Reilly. And Hawke looks forward to spending as much time as possible with Beauty.

What they're not expecting is the biggest blizzard to pass through Splendor in years.

A Very Splendor Christmas, book seventeen in the Redemption Mountain historical western romance series, is a novella with an HEA and no cliffhanger.

Visit my website for a list of characters for each series.
http://www.shirleendavies.com/character-list.html

A Very Splendor

Christmas

Chapter One

Northern Wyoming
December 1871

Glancing over his shoulder, Kev Lathan spotted the posse of six about two miles behind them. The visibility continued to deteriorate as the storm worsened. By the time he and his younger brother, Vince, reached the peak, he hoped to have lost those who followed.

As they continued the climb, their horses struggled to move through the deepening snow. Soon, they'd be above the tree line, exposing them to the posse.

Reining to his right, Kev kept them hidden within the cover of trees, continuing as fast as possible to put more distance between them and the men following. Swiping sleet from his face, he struggled to see more than ten feet ahead.

"We need cover." Vince's strained words came from his left.

Shifting toward his brother, Kev saw the deep lines of distress on Vince's face. They had to find a safe place to hide before he passed out. Searching, his gaze landed on a dark spot near a grouping of large boulders.

Scrubbing moisture from his eyes, he squinted at what appeared to be a small cave. Certain he'd found a temporary shelter, he guided his horse toward it. Before dismounting, Kev shot a look over his shoulder, confirming Vince still followed. What he saw stalled his heart.

Sliding to the ground, he rushed to his brother, catching him before he fell from his horse. Slipping an arm around Vince's waist, his shoulder holding him up, Kev walked him to the small opening in the rocks. Not as large as he'd thought, but it would have to do.

Placing him as far back as possible, Kev adjusted Vince's coat around him before rushing back to the horses to grab their bedrolls. Tucking one around his brother, he slid in next to him, throwing the other bedroll across his legs and chest.

Time passed slowly as the storm's intensity increased. Knowing he shouldn't, Kev closed his eyes, slipping into a troubled slumber.

"We can't stay here much longer or we'll freeze to death, Kev." Vince clung to the bedroll around him, his clothing doing little to protect him from the bitter cold.

They'd outrun the posse only to be trapped by the brutal storm, threatening a death as gruesome as hanging for a crime they didn't commit. Vince pulled his legs farther under him, doing all he could to conserve his diminishing body heat.

"What would you suggest?" At nineteen, a year older than Vince, Kev had taken the leadership role between the brothers. "We can't go anywhere until this storm lets up. When it does, we have to ride fast and hard to someplace far away from Colorado."

The quieter and more serious of the two, Kev detested the turn their lives had taken since the deaths of their parents. After exhausting their savings, and the bank repossessing their Missouri farm, they'd taken any jobs offered to put food in their stomachs. Living in barns, sheds, and rat infested cabins, they'd survived. Barely.

That had been more than two years ago. Since then, the brothers had traveled west, taking odd jobs, supplementing their existence by stealing the occasional chicken or cow, graduating to robbing lone travelers and the random bank.

They'd pulled their six-shooters, not once pulling the trigger. It didn't stop the sheriff of a small, southern Colorado town to accuse them of murdering a store owner and sending a posse to bring them in. Kev and Vince weren't angels. They also weren't killers.

Opening his mouth to respond, Vince's teeth chattered as he got the words out. "Where are you thinking?"

Scrubbing a hand down his icy face, Kev's red-rimmed eyes met his brother's. "I don't know yet. Maybe somewhere in Montana or the Dakotas. We don't have any history up north."

"We could ride west to Idaho or Oregon. They'd never look for us there."

"They shouldn't be looking for us at all," Kev ground out, closing his eyes when a strong gust of frigid wind blew across the shallow cave. His voice rose to be heard over the storm. "We didn't kill that shopkeeper." Rubbing his hands together, Kev blew on them for warmth. "After the storm passes, we'll decide where to go next. Then we can figure out what to do about the charges against us."

"We'll ride north to Canada. They won't follow us there."

"The weather is worse up there, Vince. We've survived all these years, sometimes with no food, shelter, or warm clothes. We'll get through this the same as always."

Falling into silence, Kev studied his brother's ashen face, worrying about the cold. Vince hadn't been well for several days. The bitter weather was making whatever he suffered from worse. He wanted to build a fire, knowing that would have to wait until the storm calmed down.

As if in answer to a prayer, the snow began to subside, gusts of wind slowing. Within a few minutes, the sky had cleared enough for Kev to leave their meager shelter.

"Stay put while I look around, Vince. I'll bring back wood for a fire."

Backtracking to where they'd left the horses, Kev sighed in relief to find they hadn't run off. Grabbing their saddlebags, he slung them over his shoulders before gathering what wood he could find.

Once Vince warmed up, they'd ride over the ridge and into Montana. He hoped to find a ranch or open land where their horses could graze.

Kev estimated they had enough jerky, hardtack, and coffee to last a few more days. Assuming they found a town, there was enough coin to buy one hot meal apiece. They needed work, anything to make more money.

Arms laden with firewood, he created a pile a few feet from Vince. Within minutes, a small fire, along with the sun's rays, began to warm the air around them. As the color returned to Vince's face, Kev dug into one of the saddlebags, pulling out two pieces of jerky.

An hour later, with their stomachs sated and warmth creeping through their limbs, they rode over the ridgeline toward Montana. Kev didn't know where they'd find shelter or their next meal. He did know they had three days before their food ran out.

A frown marred Francesca O'Reilly's features. The list of what had to be done for their wedding seemed to lengthen instead of growing shorter. One week remained before Christmas Eve services, the night she and Deputy Zeke Boudreaux would recite their vows in front of half the town.

"You look, well...overwhelmed." Amelia Newhall, one of the four women who'd traveled west with Francesca, walked into her friend's law office. Taking a seat on the other side of the desk, Amelia reached out to slide the list toward her.

"It seems to be getting longer, Amy. I must be doing something wrong."

Chuckling, she set the list down. "You're a typical woman wanting to have everything perfect. Let's see..." Amelia tapped a finger to her lips, considering what needed to get done. "I'll talk to May about the desserts, and Suzanne about the food."

May Covington, the wife of Deputy Caleb Covington, worked as the pastry chef at the Eagle's Nest restaurant. Suzanne Barnett owned the boardinghouse and restaurant. Both were providing food for the reception after Christmas services and the wedding. Most of the town women would bring additional items for the people expected. Amelia continued down the list.

"You need to meet with Allie Coulter about the final touches on your dress. You don't have to worry about candles for the church. Reverend Paige's wife, Ruth, will take care of those. May told me she also hangs several wreaths each Christmas Eve." Sliding the list back to Francesca, a knowing smile curved Amelia's mouth. "It's all going to be fine, Frannie."

Amelia had worked as a teacher in New York before Rachel Pelletier and Francesca convinced her to leave for Splendor. She now worked at the Eagle's Nest restaurant with May, prepping meals and cleaning up. Not once had she complained about the change in circumstances, preferring to think of them as learning new skills.

"I know you're right." Francesca set the list aside, and stood, grabbing her reticule from a drawer. "Are you ready for lunch?"

"I am. The restaurant was busy this morning, so I missed breakfast. That's one of the benefits of working there. Meals are free on the days we work." She joined

Francesca at the door. "Plus my small room off the kitchen. I'm able to save almost every penny I earn."

Francesca knew Amelia allowed Rose Keenan, another of the women who traveled west with them, to stay in her room. She did similar work at the boardinghouse restaurant. It included meals, but not a room.

Walking down the boardwalk to Suzanne's restaurant, they entered to find another of their friends, Georgina Wise, already seated. She worked as a nurse at the clinic, as did the last of the five women who'd come to Splendor, Carrie Galloway. She walked in a minute after Francesca and Amelia.

Carrie took a minute to look around at the decorations Suzanne had put up for Christmas. Wreaths of pine, berries, and dried fruit. Long boughs of pine studded with pine cones and red ribbons, and strings of popped corn.

"The boardinghouse is so festive with all the decorations," Carrie said, taking a seat beside Georgina. "It's been months since we've all met for lunch. Where's Rose?"

"Right here." She hurried up to them, sitting in the open chair next to Carrie. "This was such a wonderful idea."

"The only person missing is Rachel," Georgina said.

"The reason we all ended up in Splendor," Amelia added.

"She's very busy. They always have Christmas day meal for everyone at the ranch, plus several of us from town. You know we're all invited." Francesca took a sip of her coffee, setting the cup down. "Rachel has help. Still, it's a lot of work. I don't know how she does it."

The women's attention shifted toward the front door at the sound of men's voices. Deputies Hawke DeBell, Shane Banderas, and Dutch McFarlin walked in. Nodding at the ladies, the three sat at an empty table not far away.

Georgina leaned forward, lowering her voice. "Those are three very fine looking men."

Amelia nodded, one side of her mouth tilting into a soft grin. "They certainly are."

"Are they all single, Frannie?" The quietest of the five, Rose, kept her gaze diverted away from the men's table.

"I believe so." She thought of Hawke's obvious interest in Nellie Crawford, or Beauty, as many called her. As a client, Francesca knew her better than most in Splendor. To everyone else, she was a mystery.

As far as Francesca knew, he'd never formally courted her, although he spent most of his free time with the ethereal woman. Beauty didn't appear to object at his attentions.

The front door opened seconds later. Francesca's fiancé, Zeke Boudreaux, walked straight to her, bending to brush a chaste kiss across her cheek.

"Good afternoon, sweetheart." Straightening, he looked at the others. "Ladies." The women greeted him before he left to join the other deputies.

"I thought most men were anxious about getting married. Zeke doesn't seem nervous at all." Amelia gave Francesca a knowing grin.

"I'm the one who's apprehensive."

"Not an unusual reaction after he stopped calling on you the first time." Georgina had no problem bringing up the issue most of the women, including Francesca, tried to ignore. "This time, though, I don't think you should be worried. Zeke has made up his mind. The man is definitely committed to you, Frannie."

It surprised Francesca how Georgina always seemed to focus on the real issues burdening her friends. Perhaps it was her training as a nurse, which gave her insight into others. Regardless, she'd identified Francesca's fear, a concern she'd shared with no one.

"You aren't worried he'll change his mind, are you, Frannie?" Rose's brows creased in concern.

Waving a hand in the air, Francesca shook her head. "Not at all." She glanced at Georgina. "I'll admit I wasn't certain when he wanted another chance. It took a while to trust he wouldn't walk away again."

Rose lifted her gaze to Francesca. "You made the right decision, Frannie. Zeke is a wonderful man. You're fortunate to have found each other."

Glancing at the table not far away, Francesca thought back on the last year, the changes in her life which led her back to Zeke. She also thought of the dangers they'd faced from those who wanted to do them harm.

Each challenge had made their relationship stronger. Soon, they'd be saying their vows, and Francesca didn't expect any more obstacles to a shared future together.

Chapter Two

"May I escort you back to your office?" Zeke stood next to Francesca's chair. The other deputies, and all the women except Rose, had already left. Standing, she couldn't help a small smile at the look of affection between the two.

"I'd best return to the kitchen, Frannie. Suzanne will need help with the supper service."

Waiting until Rose left, Zeke held out his hand. "It's a beautiful day, Frannie. Spend a few minutes with me before getting back to your work."

Threading her fingers through his, she leaned up, kissing his chin. "There's nothing pressing at the office. I can spend as much time as you want."

He glanced up, seeing clear skies, and feeling the light breeze. They'd had a light dusting of snow the week before, which melted off within a day. Afterward, shopkeepers and townsfolk had hung wreaths from their doors, and large, red ribbons on the posts of the boardwalk.

"Hawke is going on a ride with Beauty. He invited us to join them."

Her eyes sparked with excitement. "I'd love to get away from town for a while."

Grabbing her hand, he turned them toward the livery. "Then that is what we'll do."

Hawke and Beauty were already saddling horses when they arrived. It took no time for Zeke to saddle his roan gelding, Ghost, while Noah Brandt, owner of the livery and one of the town leaders, saddled an older mare for Francesca. She stood alongside the horse, stroking her neck, whispering calming words.

Helping her into the saddle, Zeke swung on top of Ghost, edging toward Hawke. "Where to?"

"Let's ride north toward Redemption's Edge." He mentioned the Pelletier ranch, the largest in western Montana, owned by brothers Dax and Luke.

"Do you think the weather will hold?" Zeke asked.

"Best as I can tell," Hawke answered. "No rain clouds, and it's not cold enough to snow, so we should be fine."

Noah had tied blankets and great coats behind the saddles, packing canteens and jerky in the saddlebags. More than they would need for a ride of less than three hours.

They rode for a couple miles before Zeke suggested a trail to the west. Riding up a mild incline, he guided them between trees that had lost their leaves weeks before, and statuesque pines. No matter the time of year, the area around Splendor was spectacular.

Entering a clearing, Zeke reined Ghost to a stop, Hawke doing the same before helping the women to the ground. Leading them to the other side of the clearing, Zeke took a narrow path through the trees to the edge of a cliff.

"Is this the same waterfall we saw when we rode to the copper mine with Aaron and Nancy?" Francesca's friends fell in love after both traveled separately from New York a few months earlier. Aaron came to check on the copper

11

mine he owned with a partner. Nancy came to visit Francesca. They'd married before returning to the East Coast. She missed them terribly.

"The same. The second waterfall is around that point." Zeke indicated a rocky outcropping far to their right. "The copper mine is up a different trail, which is close by."

When Hawke and Beauty wandered along another trail, he turned Francesca toward him, gathering her in his arms. "In a few days, you'll be mine."

"And you'll be mine, Zeke."

Chuckling, he lowered his mouth to hers, stopping an inch away. "I've been yours for a long time, Frannie." Covering her mouth with his, he took his time, savoring every second.

They'd had little time alone since she'd accepted his proposal of marriage. Between his work and hers, plus preparations for the wedding, he'd seen her no more than an hour most days. Which was the reason he accepted Hawke's invitation to ride along.

It was Monday, with Christmas Eve occurring the following Sunday. Six more days before she'd be Mrs. Ezekiel Boudreaux.

Minutes passed before he raised his head, eyes glazed with passion staring into hers. He didn't want to be without her, not even for the few short days until their wedding. Placing one more kiss across her lips, he stepped away, continuing to grasp one hand.

"We should start moving your belongings into my house."

Wide eyes signaled her response before she spoke. "I don't have much, Zeke. Clothes and some personal items, which can be moved on Saturday. Noah said I could leave the furniture for Georgina." Her friend would be moving into the one bedroom house after Christmas.

"There will be too much going on this week to wait until the day before the wedding, sweetheart. We'll start with pictures, rugs, and your books."

Opening her mouth to respond, the first snowflake landed on her cheek. Swiping it away, she and Zeke looked upward. Neither had noticed the temperature dropping, or the dark clouds moving in. Within seconds, the wind increased, flakes coming more rapidly. Rushing to the horses, he removed the great coats Noah had packed, helping Francesca slip it on before both swung up into the saddles. A moment later, Hawke and Beauty hurried toward them.

"We need to get out of here," Hawke said, helping Beauty into the saddle.

Retracing their route down the mountain, they'd reached the junction of their trail and the northern road into Splendor when Francesca's attention caught on a flash of red.

"Hawke, Zeke, wait."

Stopping, she slid to the ground, rushing toward what she'd seen. Francesca dropped to her knees next to a small mound covered in what appeared to be a red blanket. Beauty knelt beside her, lifting the wool covering.

"Oh, my." The air left Francesca's lungs.

13

A boy and girl, not more than seven or eight years old, lay together, arms wrapped protectively around each other. Their only protection was the tattered red blanket. Reaching out, she touched the boy's forehead, gasping when he reared up, arms swinging at Francesca.

Beauty turned toward the men, who stood a few feet away. "We may need your help."

Grasping the boy's wrists, Zeke held them in a firm, gentle grip. "Calm down. We're going to help you."

Panicked eyes whipped between the four adults, landing on the girl next to him. Draping his too thin body over hers, the boy's expression turned fierce.

"I won't let you hurt her."

"We aren't going to hurt either of you," Hawke said, his voice soothing. "What's your name?"

The boy's gaze bore into Hawke's. "I'm not saying."

Letting out a sigh, Beauty touched the boy's shoulder. "We're here to help. How long has it been since you've eaten?"

"I don't remember."

"Shep?"

"I'm here, Maisy."

"It's cold and I'm hungry."

Glancing at Beauty, his eyes beseeched hers. "Do you have anything my sister can eat?"

Hearing the question, Maisy sat up, scooting closer to Shep. "Who are they?"

"I'm Beauty, and this is Francesca." She nodded toward the men. "This is Hawke, and the man next to him is Zeke."

Standing, Hawke walked to his saddlebags, pulling out a small tin of hardtack. Grabbing his canteen, he dropped back down. "This, and water, is all we have. We'll get you some real food in town." Looking up at the sky, his gaze swung to Beauty. "The storm is worsening. We need to get going."

Handing each child a piece of hardtack, Hawke scooped Maisy into his arms. "She can ride with you, Beauty."

Mounting, she took the girl into her arms, settling her in front. Zeke grabbed the dirty blanket, handing it to Beauty to wrap around Maisy. Grasping Shep under his arms, Zeke placed him in the saddle, swinging up behind him.

"Let's go."

The storm hadn't worsened to the point they couldn't see. Compared to most, this one was mild, the wind swirling but not yet gusting.

It didn't take long to reach Splendor. Zeke rode straight to the clinic.

"I don't need no doctor," Shep complained, trying to get away from Zeke as he dragged him to the front door.

Watching her brother's shenanigans, Maisy chose to walk peacefully beside Beauty. "He don't like being told what to do."

Following Zeke and Shep inside, Beauty brushed the snow off Maisy. "Few people do."

"What do we have here?" Doctor Charles Worthington, Rachel Pelletier's uncle, walked down the stairs, stopping feet from them.

"We found these children outside of town. Can you check them over, Doc?" Zeke asked.

"Sure can. Bring them in here." Opening the door of an examination room, the doctor motioned for them to enter ahead of him. Zeke stopped next to Charles.

"While you're looking them over, I'm going to McCall's to get some food. I think it's been a while since they've eaten."

"You go on, Zeke. I'll be finished checking them over by the time you get back."

Sitting at a table in an upstairs room of the clinic, Shep and Maisy packed food into their mouths, barely swallowing before adding more. During the examination, it had become clear they'd been on the verge of starvation. Beauty had forced herself to hold back tears, seeing the way their skin stretched over their bones.

Doc fought to keep them from eating so much they became ill, finally removing the food after a fourth of it had disappeared. "You let that settle a while. If you don't get sick, you can have more in a bit." Leaving them, he joined Hawke, Beauty, Zeke, and Francesca just outside the room. "What do you plan to do with them?"

Splendor didn't have an orphanage or services for children with nowhere to go. The Pelletiers and a couple other ranch families had taken in orphans in the past, but it had been a few years.

"Until we find them homes, Shep can stay with me, and Maisy with Francesca," Zeke offered.

"They aren't going to want to be separated, Zeke. I don't mind Maisy staying with me, but the children aren't going to like the arrangements."

Crossing his arms, Zeke stared up at the ceiling. "Nick and Suzanne might be willing to take them in. They have a big house. And it's just them and their son, Newt."

"Why not Isabella and Travis Dixon?" Doc asked. "She loves children, and their house has two bedrooms. After Christmas, they can be taken to the orphanage in Big Pine."

"Orphanage..." Beauty said the word as if it were a curse. "Have you ever seen it, Doctor?"

"I have." Charles scrubbed a hand over his face, glancing back into the room where Shep and Maisy talked among themselves. "The owner reminds me of Suzanne Barnett. Good woman, but never enough funds to do all she plans. Last time I was there, she had more children than beds. Clare and I send money a few times a year, but not enough to get them a bigger house. Sheriff Sterling said the town leaders have been talking about adding on to the place for years. Nothing's happened yet." Removing his spectacles, he rubbed his eyes. "Are you certain they're orphans? When we asked Shep during the examination, he didn't answer."

17

"Good question, Doc. I've been wondering how they got north of Splendor. The stage doesn't come into town or leave using that trail." Zeke stared at the table, seeing both children with their arms folded on the table, their heads resting on top. "They're exhausted. Let's get them to my house, Frannie. It's time we learned about their parents, how they got to Splendor, and where they were headed."

Chapter Three

"You're certain the stage will reach Splendor before Christmas Eve?" Dorothea O'Reilly held her hand up to shield her eyes as the driver secured luggage to the top of the stage.

The temperature had dropped since leaving Denver, and according to one of the passengers, it would continue to plummet as they traveled into Montana. Dorothea didn't care about slight inconveniences such as the weather. She'd packed plenty of warm clothes, including a fur muff for her hands, which matched her fur hat.

"We'll be in Splendor on Saturday, ma'am. You should be fine."

Dorothea wasn't certain she agreed, but had no power over the weather or route they'd be taking. It had been an arduous journey, already taking longer than expected. Thank goodness she'd planned for such delays in the schedule.

Climbing into the coach, Dorothea nodded at the new passengers, offering a small smile to the younger gentleman who'd traveled with her since Denver. A private person, he'd shared little about himself or his destination. The silence hadn't bothered her. She spent the time writing letters or reading one of several dime novels.

Settling herself on the seat, Dorothea reached into a small satchel, retrieving her spectacles and latest novel. *Seth Jones, The Captives of the Frontier.*

"I've read that one several times and always enjoy it."

Glancing next to her at a woman about her age, Dorothea smiled. "This is my first time. So far, it's quite compelling."

Reaching into her own travel bag, the woman pulled out her own book, holding it up. *Malaeska, The Indian Wife of the White Hunter.* "This is a new one for me. You're welcome to borrow it after I'm finished."

"Thank you. I have others, and you're welcome to borrow any of them."

After brief introductions, the women fell into a comfortable silence at the same time the driver shouted their departure and the stage left Cheyenne.

Dorothea settled against the seat, trying to concentrate on the novel as the stage bounced over the rutted trail. After a while, she gave up, switching her attention to the other passengers.

There was the young man who'd been traveling with her since she boarded the train in New York. They hadn't sat with each other for most of it, and she knew little about him. Not even his final destination. Dorothea wished she'd asked more questions.

Noticing the tired faces, she decided to take a chance. "Where is everyone headed?"

All eyes flickered to her, the woman beside her smiling. "I'm visiting my daughter and her family in Big Pine. It's the territorial capital. This is my first trip out west. It's been quite exciting."

"My son and I are going to Boise," a man who looked to be in his late twenties said. "I have a job at the new prison. My brother and his family already live there."

"Mama is dead." The young boy blurted it out, surprising the others. Putting an arm around his son, his father drew him to his side. The announcement quieted those in the coach.

A few minutes passed before Dorothea looked at the man who'd been heading west since she boarded the railroad in New York. "And what is your final destination?"

Lifting his head, the man's gaze, void of expression, caught hers. To Dorothea, he had what her husband would call distant eyes. No emotion, nothing to indicate the beliefs behind the cold expression. When she thought he wouldn't answer, he spoke.

"I haven't decided."

Kev Lathan snuck around one side of the farmhouse, rising to look through each window. Vince did the same on the other side. If their luck held, they'd find the house empty, giving them an opportunity to grab food and supplies before leaving.

Meeting at the back door, Kev took one more look around. "The place is empty. Could be they left to get supplies."

"Or maybe it's abandoned. Let's go inside and look around."

Kev motioned for Vince to enter the house. Following behind him, both with their guns drawn, Kev took the hallway to the right while Vince went straight toward the front of the house. The early morning sun streamed through the windows, giving the house an almost haunted feel.

The two had already agreed no one would get hurt. The fact was, if they encountered someone inside, the brothers would run.

Finding the downstairs empty, Vince took the stairs two at a time. Returning a minute later, he shook his head. "The place is deserted. Furniture is here, but their clothes are gone, nothing on the dresser or in the drawers. Books are missing from shelves, and there aren't any photographs."

"Let's check the kitchen." Kev took long strides to the back, concerned the cupboards would be empty. Pulling open drawers and doors, they found little. "Tins of flour, sugar, and coffee."

Vince held up another tin. "Biscuits." In his other hand was a canning jar. "Jam. Maybe there's a root cellar." Setting the items down, he hurried outside while Kev continued to search the kitchen.

Setting what he found on the counter, Kev estimated they had enough food to make it a few more days when Vince returned. In his hands were jars of peaches, berries, and corn.

"We can live weeks off of what is in the cellar." He didn't have to mention the horses that grazed in a pasture near the barn. "Whoever lived here must've left in a hurry, or ran out of room in their wagon to carry everything. We should consider hiding out here for a while."

Jaw tensing, Kev stepped to one of the windows, then another, scanning the area around the house. Taking another tour of the house, he ended up at the front windows, still studying the land. Vince moved next to him, understanding his brother's caution.

"We rest here two to three days, then move on. One of us keeps watch at all times. The horses, saddled and ready to go, will be close by. We'll stuff the saddlebags with as much as we can." Kev placed his hands on his hips, letting out a slow breath. "If the owners abandoned this place, it won't be long until someone from the bank rides out to look around."

Answering with a grin, Vince opened the jar of peaches. Scooping one out, he popped it into his mouth, handing the jar to Kev.

Saying nothing while he ate the peach halves, Kev began to relax. "Staying here will give us time to explore the area. I figure there must be a town nearby."

"We've got weather moving in. I'll ride west, see what's out that way."

Kev noticed the color in his brother's face, the way his eyes lit up. A couple days, and getting off the mountain, had made a big difference to the illness plaguing Vince.

"Go ahead. Get a look around before the storm comes through. Take food with you, and be careful. We don't know if the sheriff in Colorado got a judge to approve a wanted poster on us. If he did, there may be men out there after us."

"I'll be careful, Kev. I don't expect to be gone more than a few hours. Enough time to see if there's a town west of here. We know there's nothing south. We don't know about north or east."

"I should ride with you, Vince."

"It'd be better for you to go east a ways. We should pack our saddlebags with extra food. In case we return to find the owners have returned."

Kev took a slow look around the house before heading out the back door. "Let's get the food packed away and take off. I'm looking forward to a decent night's sleep inside a real house."

"You and me both, brother."

Splendor

Francesca sat on the bench, Isabella Dixon next to her, watching Shep and Maisy throw snowballs into the creek. Wearing gloves and fur hats, the women had pulled their coats tight to stifle the cold breeze.

"I know it's almost Christmas, and I'm certain you're busy with preparations, so don't feel you have to help, Isabella."

"I have enough time to watch the children, Frannie. You can bring them over when you leave for work, or I can come to your house."

"They're actually staying at Zeke's place since he has two bedrooms. I'll ask him if he wants to walk them to your house in the morning. As I said, it's only until after Christmas. Unless we can find a local family to take them in, we'll need to take them to the orphanage in Big Pine."

Isabella's face fell. "Do you know anything about the orphanage?"

"Doc Worthington and his wife, Clare, know the woman who operates it. They also make donations. I'm hoping Clare will go with us if we have to take the children there."

"May I go with you? I wouldn't mind meeting the woman and touring the home."

"Hawke and Beauty will be riding along. We'd love for you to accompany us. It's just..." Francesca's voice trailed off.

"You don't want to think about leaving Shep and Maisy there, right?"

Francesca watched the children playing in the snow, holding out hope there'd be other choices for them. There were still several questions needing answers. She and Zeke would be asking those tonight after supper.

"Yes. Maybe I'll change my mind once I see the home and meet the administrator."

"Have you spoken with Reverend and Ruth Paige about them?"

Francesca swept the light dusting of snow from her coat, shaking her head. "No, I haven't."

"You should consider meeting with them. They may know of a couple who'd take in the children." A wistful look appeared in Isabella's eyes. "I would love to have them, but Travis won't discuss it."

Cocking her head to one side, Francesca waited, but Isabella said nothing more. She knew there was a story behind his decision, but wouldn't ask.

"I'll speak with Ruth this week."

Standing, Isabella shook the lower half of her coat, dislodging the snow. "I know you need to get to your office. Don't worry about the children. I'll take care of Shep and Maisy for as long as you need."

"Thank you. I don't know what we would've done if you weren't able to watch them."

A sadness washed over her features. "Travis works at the Pelletier ranch, getting home late each night. We have no children of our own, so I don't have much to keep me busy. I'm not complaining, just letting you know I have more than enough time to take care of Maisy and Shep."

"Miss Frannie," Maisy yelled, a snowball in her small hand. "Come and play with us."

A snowball landed at Francesca's feet a moment before one hit her coat. Laughing, she bent down to scoop up a handful of snow. Packing it into a ball, she tossed it at Maisy before making another, this one landing on Shep.

When another hit Isabella in the chest, the battle commenced in earnest, each of the four a perfect target. Laughter followed each toss, the children dashing around to find better positions and more snow.

Before long, all four were covered in icy flakes, the women's hats askew. Their laughter brought others, until a dozen people stood a few feet away. Breaking through the small crowd, Zeke stood with hands on his hips.

Unable to stand aside and watch, he moved closer, creating two large balls. Stalking toward them, he let loose, one hitting Shep, the other, Francesca. Surprised, each shrieked, noticing him for the first time.

Others joined in, unstructured bedlam consuming the area. Laughter rang through the small crowd, while creating the most enjoyable chaos anyone could remember in a long time.

Chapter Four

Redemption's Edge Ranch

"Luke, do you have this handled?" The older of the two Pelletier brothers, Dax, swung into the saddle. They'd been working with Travis and Billy Zales to break enough horses to fulfill the latest Army contract.

"We can finish this, Dax." Luke didn't spare him another glance before getting back to work.

"Billy?" The young man looked at his boss, one of the men who'd saved him and other orphans from starving to death years before.

"Boss?"

"Who's with Shining Star?" Dax mentioned the Blackfoot maiden, pregnant from an attack by a Crow brave. Her grandfather, Running Bear, had brought her to the Pelletier ranch to hide her from a Crow raiding party. When first arriving at the ranch, Billy was the one person she felt comfortable around.

A guilty expression crossed the young ranch hand's face. "Rachel, Ginny, and Lydia said she could work with them until we were finished."

"That isn't what we agreed to," Dax reminded him.

"I know, boss." Placing fisted hands on his hips, he looked between the brothers. "I'm a wrangler. I need to work with the horses, not follow some woman around."

Humor flickered in Luke's eyes as the corners of Dax's mouth twitched. "I understand. We all do. Our agreement with Running Bear was for you to be the one to protect his granddaughter. I intend to keep that promise. Finish up here, then find Shining Star." Moving a few yards away, Dax shifted in the saddle. "We expect you all to be at Christmas Eve services. Billy, Shining Star will be going with us."

Billy groaned, giving Dax a sharp nod.

"We'll be going into town and returning together." Luke clasped him on the shoulder. "All the men will be watching out for the women and children. Now, let's get this done."

Billy continued to work alongside Travis and Luke, his mind on the beautiful Blackfoot woman. No one understood his true feelings for her. They didn't know he'd fallen in love with her during his first visit to the Blackfoot village. At the time, he didn't know her affections had already been given to one of the Blackfoot warriors.

He and several men from Redemption's Edge had been at the village when her brave died during a Crow raid. Her grief had been heartbreaking to watch.

The pregnancy resulted after a Crow brave found her alone, then forced himself on her. She'd escaped, but not before the damage had been done. When the Blackfoot women learned of her condition and how it came about, they'd shown their displeasure. Shunning her, the women made it impossible for Shining Star to remain in the village.

Running Bear's decision to seek refuge for his granddaughter at the Pelletier ranch had taken everyone by surprise. Even so, she'd been welcomed.

Billy had been by her side almost every day, watching for threats, making certain she came to no harm. Over the months, he'd spent countless hours teaching her English while she taught him the Blackfoot language. Their time together had deepened his feelings for her. Feelings Shining Star didn't seem to return.

It had become too difficult to be with her for hours each day, knowing she'd never be his. He needed distance, someone else to take over guarding her.

Billy intended to wait until after Christmas before requesting a meeting with Dax. He was certain the elder Pelletier brother would understand and provide a different man to protect Shining Star. Running Bear would accept the change, allowing Billy to return to the work he loved.

Splendor

Hawke's steps were slow as he escorted Beauty back to her house after a late lunch. She'd slipped her arm through his the instant they'd left McCall's, staying close to his side. Ever since the threat to her life several months earlier, she'd welcomed his visits.

Over time, his intentions toward the stunning woman had changed. She'd broken through the solid wall which kept him safe from more pain. He didn't delude himself. No matter how much he enjoyed her company, Hawke couldn't allow himself to foresee a future with any woman.

Reaching her front door, he turned her to face him. "Thank you for joining me."

A slow grin spread across her face, ending in a sparkling smile. "You know I enjoy the time we spend together."

Something in her eyes had him lowering his face, hesitating a moment before brushing his lips over hers. He'd kissed her before. Brief, tentative touches of his mouth to hers. Beauty had never pulled away.

This time, however, the only woman to stir his blood since his wife died leaned into him, hands gripping his shoulders. When she parted her lips, he delved inside, groaning at the intense rush of desire.

Her actions today were clear. She wanted more, wouldn't turn him away if he went further. Hawke couldn't deny he wanted the same. On her front porch, in the middle of the day, wasn't the place, and now wasn't the time.

Releasing a slow, calming breath, he set her several inches away. "I have to get to the jail."

Swiping strands of hair from her face, she lifted glazed eyes to meet his. "Of course." Moistening her lips, she inched away. "Um...thank you again for lunch."

Hawke DeBell sat outside the jail in the waning late afternoon sun, watching people scurry about as the falling snow changed from a slow dusting to a genuine storm. Not too strong, but enough wind and snow to encourage those outside to complete their errands and return home. Unlike them, he had nowhere to go.

Not that he didn't have a place to sleep at night. Hawke and another deputy, Shane Banderas, rented one of Noah's houses. Theirs was much the same as Zeke's with two bedrooms.

"Good afternoon, Deputy."

Recognizing the voice, he lifted his head from whittling a small piece of wood to see Alana Hanrahan. She worked at Finn's, the newest saloon in Splendor. The deputies suspected she offered more than serving drinks to the customers. She'd made her interest in Hex Boudreaux obvious before he'd married Christina McKenna. Lately, Alana's interest had turned to him.

He touched the brim of his hat. "Afternoon, Miss Hanrahan. What brings you out in this weather?"

Alana's face flushed a little, the corners of her mouth lifting in a wry grin. "I saw you sitting out here, Deputy, and thought you'd enjoy a visitor."

"Well, that's real nice of you." Sliding the wood into a pocket, Hawke stood. "It's getting cold out here, and the storm is worsening. Why don't I walk you back to Finn's before I start my rounds?"

"I would be most grateful for your company." She slipped her arm through his. "The road is a little icy, don't you think?"

No, he didn't, but he kept the opinion to himself. Crossing the street, and continuing along the boardwalk, he left her at the entrance to Finn's. The sound of the tinny piano wafted outside, giving the saloon a hint of gaiety on a cold, early evening.

"Stay warm, Miss Hanrahan."

"You do the same. Thank you for bringing me home...Hawke." Flashing him a bright smile, she pushed through the doors.

Not staying to reflect on her use of his given name or the enticing smile, one he'd seen many times in his life, Hawke continued along the boardwalk. Acknowledging those who passed by him, his mind went to the woman who'd held his interest for months. The woman he'd kissed less than an hour before.

Beauty arrived in Splendor not long before him. After years of mourning the deaths of his wife and children, Hawke had felt the first stirrings of desire. The guilt had made him sick.

He still loved his late wife, Fiona. Would always love and miss her. The dream he had as a young man of seventeen had been buried along with his family after returning from the war. Their lives had ended at the hands of ex-Confederate raiders. He'd been a captain for the Confederacy, the betrayal of those he may have fought alongside burned deep.

33

Instead of rebuilding his farm, settling on familiar soil, Hawke had become a bounty hunter. It had taken time, but after countless miles, those who'd murdered his family suffered a similar fate. Their deaths at his hand hadn't cleared the anger, or the pain in his heart. Time and distance had lessened the anguish to a throbbing ache.

Meeting the stunning woman with white blonde hair, silver gray eyes, and a flowing walk had done more in a few short months to ease his pain than dozens of bottles of whiskey. Guilt, though, had proven to be a difficult beast to ignore. How could he love another woman when his heart still belonged to Fiona?

Forcing his thoughts elsewhere, he reached the front door of the Emporium, admiring the display behind the front window. Several oil and kerosene lamps cast a warm glow on the tall pine tree laden with gold and red ribbons, strings of berries, and colorful wood ornaments. Knowing Josie Lucero and Olivia McCord would be home by now, he checked the door, settling his hand on the butt of his gun when it opened.

Stepping inside, he glanced around, listening for voices from the back. "Josie? Olivia? Anyone inside?"

Getting no answer, he pulled his six-shooter from its holster. He didn't try to soften the sound of his boots on the wood floor. Stepping around a display of toys for Christmas, he continued to the back, stopping at a scraping sound.

"Whoever's in here, come out with your hands up." Hawke took several more steps toward the back. When the odd scraping sounded again, his pace sped up until he stood at the entrance of the storage area. Holding the six-shooter in front of him, Hawke swung into the room. When his gaze landed on the intruder, he froze.

Huddled in a corner was a young boy. No coat, hat, or gloves, his lips had turned a deep blue, his body shaking from the cold. Holstering his gun, he grabbed one of the blankets folded on an upper shelf. Hawke rushed to the child, covering his emaciated body.

Sweeping him into his arms, he rushed out the back door. Taking a path behind the buildings, he knocked at the kitchen entrance to Suzanne's boardinghouse restaurant. When the door opened, Rose stood inside, jaw dropping,

"Oh, my. Please, come inside." Closing the door, she motioned to one of two chairs at a small table. "I'll warm some milk." Rose returned to them a minute later with a thick slice of bread slathered with butter and jam before pouring the milk into a cup. "Do you need another blanket?"

Holding the boy on his lap, Hawke touched his face, feeling the heat. "He's burning up. I need to get him to the clinic."

Bending down, Rose brushed brown hair from his forehead. "What's your name?"

Holding the bread in both hands, jam spread around his mouth, his wide, dark eyes met hers. Instead of answering, he took another bite, as if she might take the food away.

"I'll get Suzanne."

"No. The milk and bread is fine, Rose." Standing, Hawke hugged the boy to his chest. "I want to get to the clinic before the storm gets worse."

Rushing to the counter, she cut another thick slice of bread, wrapping it in a towel. "Take this with you."

"Thanks, Rose."

Leaving through the front entrance, Hawke avoided wagons and riders on his way to the clinic. It was growing late, the air frigid. The last rays of the sun had disappeared an hour earlier. The boy burrowed farther into his chest, his body seeking warmth to calm his shivers.

Hawke blew out a relieved sigh at the light coming from inside the clinic. Shoving open the door with his boot, he rushed inside.

"Doc?"

Clay McCord came down the stairs, his face drawn, eyes showing his exhaustion. Pointing to an examination room, he lit three lanterns inside the room.

Pulling down the blanket, Clay looked up at Hawke. "Who is he?"

"I don't know. Found him in the Emporium during my rounds. He was huddled in the storage room without a jacket, hat, or gloves."

Clay's eyes widened at the name of the store his wife, Olivia, owned with Josie Lucero. Continuing to check the boy, both men winced at his gaunt appearance, the way his eyes bulged from hollowed sockets. Then there were the scrapes, cuts, and bruises.

"I took him to the boardinghouse. Rose gave him bread with jam and warm milk."

"Rose is a good woman." Clay cleaned the cuts, his lips drawn into a thin line. "No fractures. Wonder where his parents are." Catching the boy watching him, he bent lower. "What's your name, son?"

The boy's skittish gaze swung to Hawke before returning to Clay.

"It's all right," Hawke said. "You can tell the doc and me."

Continuing to stare between the two men, he worried his bottom lip. "Joel."

"Do you know your last name?" Hawke asked.

Joel didn't respond this time, preferring to stare across the room at the cabinets filled with medicines and other concoctions.

"How old are you?"

He held up four fingers at the same time as answering. "Four."

"Well, Joel, I'm going to fix you up. You'll stay at the clinic tonight, then we're going to find a place for you to stay until you get your strength back."

Joel nodded, the hope on the young boy's face creating a crack in Hawke's heart.

"Do you know how we can find your parents?" Doc's question had Joel almost jumping from the bed before both men held him down. "That's all right. We won't talk about them now."

"I want my brother and sister."

Hawke's brows drew together. "Were they in the store with you?"

A vigorous shake of Joel's head provided the answer.

Hawke tried again. "Where are they?"

"I don't know." Features sagging with sadness, he wouldn't meet their gazes. "Ma and Pa left them on the trail before we got to town."

This got both the men's attention. "What are their names, Joel?" Hawke asked.

"Pa and Ma said I shouldn't talk about the family."

Hawke set a hand on the boy's frail shoulder. "Well now, that's good advice. Except this time, we're trying to get you back with your family. Maybe your brother and sister are already here in Splendor. If so, we might know them."

Catching his lower lip between his teeth, Joel cast his worried gaze around the room. "Ma and Pa will get mad at me. They'll punish me."

Clay and Hawke exchanged looks, the doctor giving a slow shake of his head. They'd ask more about his parents later.

"For now, let's see if we can find your brother and sister. Doc and I have lots of friends in town. If they're here, someone will know about them."

Long moments later, Joel turned his head toward Hawke, letting out a shaky breath. "Their names are Shep and Maisy."

Chapter Five

Hawke could smell the delicious aroma of supper as he stood on Zeke's front porch. From the laughter, he guessed Francesca, Shep, and Maisy were also inside. He'd met them when Zeke had brought them to the jail, introducing the children to the deputies while checking wanted posters. No one had heard of the Waltons, or of a couple looking for their lost children.

Knocking, Hawke stepped back when Zeke opened the door. "Good evening, Hawke. Come inside. Have you had supper, because Francesca made plenty."

"Smells wonderful. If you're sure there's enough..." His gaze locked on Shep and Maisy, who played on the floor. Hawke hadn't decided how to approach the news their younger brother had been found.

"I'll set a place for you."

"Good evening, Frannie."

"Hello, Hawke. I'm glad you came by. As always, I've made more than the four of us can eat."

He moved to stand next to her, lowering his voice. "Have you found a home for the children?"

"Nothing yet. Isabella would love to take them in, but Travis has made it clear he doesn't want children. I spoke to Ruth Paige this morning. She's going to let others know about the children. If no one responds, I'm afraid we'll be taking them to the orphanage in Big Pine after Christmas."

Taking the whiskey Zeke handed him, Hawke cleared his throat. "I found a little boy hiding in the Emporium on my rounds tonight. Emaciated, no warm clothes. Said his parents left him outside of town and drove off." He glanced at Shep and Maisy. "He told Doc McCord and me they'd dumped his older brother and sister a ways out on the trail to Splendor."

Francesca's spoon hovered above the pot. "Did he provide names?"

"Shep and Maisy."

Her eyes grew wide. "My God. There's another brother."

Zeke's jaw clenched. "A third child. How could parents do that to them?"

Taking a slow swallow of his whiskey, Hawke shook his head. "I witnessed abandonment a good many times right after the war."

"It's been six years." Francesca's strained voice indicated the extent of her irritation. "Shep was born at the end of the war, and Maisy a year later. How old is their brother?"

"Joel is four. Doc is keeping him overnight, but I need a place for him tomorrow. Do you think Isabella would watch him? I'll pay for the food and buy him clothes."

Francesca's features softened. "I'm certain she would. We should tell Shep and Maisy about Joel."

Sliding an arm around her waist, Zeke leaned close. "After supper."

"They won't be able to see him tonight. Doc McCord wants him to rest." Swallowing the last of his whiskey, Hawke's face darkened. "They need to be prepared to see Joel. He's lost a good deal of weight. His skin is sallow and eyes sunken. I doubt he would've lasted out the week if I hadn't found him in the Emporium. He had a jar of hard candies in front of him. Those may have been the only food he's had in days. If I find their parents..." Hawke's jaw hardened. He didn't have to finish for Zeke and Francesca to know what he meant.

Beauty set down the drinks in front of two cowboys she'd never seen in the Grand Palace before. Not one to make idle conversation, she tended to visualize stories about people in her mind. Rough looking with scruffy beards, she guessed they were from down south. Texas, maybe.

Noting the gunbelts carrying two six-shooters each, she revised her imaginings. These weren't cowhands. They were gunfighters, or those hunting men for their bounty.

Walking away, her mind wandered to Hawke. He'd been a bounty hunter before arriving in Splendor. Beauty knew some of his story.

While he'd been stuck guarding her when her life had been threatened, he'd shared about the loss of his wife and twin boys. She marveled at how he'd controlled his emotions, talking as if he were describing a neighbor's family and not his own. In contrast, Beauty had swiped tears from her face, chest squeezing at his pain. She'd asked no questions, but yearned to know more about his past.

Stopping at the bar, she set down the tray, resting her arms on the sleek wood. He hadn't come to her house or the Palace since their kiss yesterday afternoon. Twenty-four hours. It amazed her how much she missed him. In all her time with Kyle Forshew, not once had she missed him to the extent she did Hawke.

"Looks to me we're going to have a slow night, Beauty." Ruby leaned on the bar next to her, motioning to the bartender for a drink. "You might as well go home."

"It's early, Ruby. Maybe I should wait a while, see if more customers come in."

"No. You return home, Beauty. We're fine for tonight." Picking up the glass, Ruby emptied it before walking away.

Staring after her, she shoved away from the bar, offering a drawn smile to the bartender. Everyone who worked for Ruby knew Beauty didn't need the money. Coming to the Palace most afternoons gave her purpose, forcing her out of the house for a few hours.

Fetching her coat, hat, and gloves from a closet in the back, she left by the side door. The frigid air hit her face, encouraging Beauty to quicken her pace between the Palace and her house.

A smile brightened her face when the house came into view. It might not be much when compared to those in larger cities, but the two bedroom home was hers. Rather, she rented it from the owners, Noah and Abby Brandt.

Getting closer, Beauty's gaze landed on a figure sitting in a chair on the front porch. *Hawke DeBell.*

Steps faltering, she stopped, unable to determine whether or not he'd seen her. When he raised his hand in welcome, she let out a breath and continued to the porch.

"Early night, Beauty?" He didn't stand up, nor tip his hat, two courtesies common to him. His face looked drawn, tired, and something else. Worry, perhaps.

Wrapping both arms around her waist, she leaned against a post. "Seems the weather has kept the customers away. What are you doing here, Hawke?"

Shoving up, he stepped closer. "May I come inside?"

Head tiling to one side, her brows drew together. "Of course." Shoving the door open, they shed their coats, hats, and gloves. She headed to the stove. "Coffee?"

A weary smile broke across his face. "Please. In exchange, I'll get a fire started for you. It's a good trade, Beauty. You should take it."

Chuckling, she shook her head, making a fresh pot. "I think it's an excellent trade. Please, sit down, Deputy."

Not much had changed since he'd been inside her house. A vase filled with pine branches, and a few homemade Christmas decorations...simple additions, yet they added more warmth to what was already a welcoming home.

It took little time to start a fire in two of the three stoves Noah had installed in the house. The chill in the kitchen and living room faded within minutes as the smell of coffee wafted toward where Hawke sat in one of two overstuffed chairs.

"Here you are." Beauty handed him a cup, then took a seat in the other chair. Waiting as he sipped the coffee, she studied his profile, much as she did whenever close to him. "What really brings you to my house so late at night?"

"It's not that late."

"I'd say nine o'clock is a little late for a social call." Beauty cradled her cup in both hands, the warmth spreading through her.

"Do I need a reason to come by, even this late?"

Feeling heat creep up her face, Beauty shook her head. "No, you don't. I want you to always feel welcome."

Her honesty seared through him, the truth in her words making him grin. "I left Zeke's house after supper and found myself walking in this direction."

She laughed. "It's less than thirty feet between her house and mine."

Rubbing his brow, he stretched out his legs, taking another sip of coffee. "This evening, I found Shep and Maisy's younger brother, Joel, hiding in the Emporium."

Sitting up, she placed her cup on the table, lips pressed together. "Was he all right?"

"No. Starving, with no warm clothes. He's only four."

Covering her mouth, her eyes began to tear. "Where is he now?"

"At the clinic. Doc McCord is with him." Scrubbing a hand down his face, Hawke stared straight ahead. "I'd witnessed a great deal of cruelty during the war and after.

More than you'd believe possible. After six years, I still have a hard time understanding how some parents treat their children. They dropped him off to take care of himself. The same way they dumped Shep and Maisy north of town. I swear I'm going to find their parents and make them regret their actions."

Standing, she sat on the arm of Hawke's chair, placing a hand on his shoulder. "Maybe it would be best to let them go. The children will be better off with a family who will love and protect them."

Locking his gaze on hers, he ran a hand through his thick, coal-black hair. "Who's going to take in three children? Francesca and Zeke are trying to find a home for them, but the odds aren't good. If no one wants them, we'll be forced to take them to the orphanage in Big Pine."

Long moments passed in silence before Beauty spoke again.

"I'll take them."

Sliding his legs back under him, Hawke shifted in the chair to pin her with an incredulous stare. "You'll what?"

Rising from her perch on the arm of his chair, she paced to the other side of the room before turning to face him. "I'll take the children. All three of them. I have plenty of money and no other responsibilities. The children can share one of the bedrooms until Noah has a house with three bedrooms available to rent."

She watched Hawke, whose expression gave away nothing. His dark golden eyes locked on hers, yet they told her nothing of what he thought. Tapping a finger against her lips, she bit her lower lip in concentration.

"I'll quit my job at the Palace. I—" She stopped when Hawke abruptly stood.

"Do you have any idea what it takes to raise one child?"

Eyes wide, she gave a slow shake of her head.

"You're talking about three, Beauty. Three children we know nothing about. How do you know they weren't raised to be thieves and pickpockets? How do we know their parents aren't camped somewhere outside of town, waiting for them to return with whatever they've stolen?"

His voice never rose, nor did he move closer to her. Even as his questions sounded ridiculous, she knew they were reasonable. Licking her lips, she crossed her arms in front of her.

"We *don't* know. Not yet, anyway." Walking toward him, she lowered herself onto the sofa a couple feet away. Positioning herself on the edge, hands clasped in front of her, Beauty's voice stayed as calm as his. "There are questions we need to ask the children. If their answers seem reasonable, I want to take them into my home."

Rubbing his forehead, Hawke pulled his gaze from hers to stare at the floor. "Are you prepared for the pain if you lose them?"

Tilting her head, her voice softened. "What do you mean?"

"The pain. Do you have any idea the agony you'll experience if you grow to love the children and lose any of them?"

46

She'd reached out to rest her hand on his hand, but he stepped away. Beauty hadn't thought that far ahead. Nor had she considered how Hawke would react to her taking in children. How this would remind him of his own losses. The obvious pain on his face made her mistake all too clear.

The idea of losing any of them hadn't occurred to her. It *had* occurred to him. When he didn't say more, she leaned toward him.

"Hawke?"

Instead of answering, he walked to the door, grabbing his hat. "I need to leave."

Jumping up, she followed him to the door. "I'm sorry, Hawke. I wasn't thinking. Are you all right?"

Hand on the knob, he looked down at her. "Fine."

Beauty didn't believe he was all right, but wouldn't push for more now. "Thank you for letting me know about the children."

Already down the front steps, he turned back, a resigned expression on his face. "Goodnight, Beauty."

Chapter Six

Dorothea O'Reilly drew back the thick leather covering, taking worried looks out the stage window at the unwanted riders. The driver had already alerted them to a group of Shoshone about a hundred yards away. They tracked the stage's movements, but didn't approach.

He'd warned them of the Shoshone tribe before pulling out of the last swing station, where they'd changed horses and taken five minutes to attend to personal needs. Most times, they allowed stagecoaches to pass near their lands without incident. On the rare occasion, a renegade group would attack, killing or injuring before retreating back to their village.

"Don't worry, dear." The woman beside her reached out, patting Dorothea's hand. "You'll be getting to your daughter's wedding as planned."

Seeing the Shoshone continue to pace the stage, Dorothea wasn't as certain. They were to arrive in Big Pine that evening, rest for a few hours, then continue on to Splendor on Saturday. Unless more passengers boarded in the territorial capital, she might be traveling alone the last leg of her trip.

She shot a glance at the man who'd been traveling the same distance as her, wondering as to his final destination. He'd been vague when asked, divulging nothing about himself or his plans.

"I hope you're right. She is to marry on Sunday afternoon, and doesn't know I'm coming. It will be quite a surprise for Frannie. Did I tell you my daughter's a lawyer?"

The other woman glanced at her, hiding a smirk. "You may have mentioned it. I'm certain you're quite proud of her."

"Oh, yes. My husband and I are quite proud of her achievements." Not quite true, but her husband was slowly changing his view on their daughter. Dorothea wished her husband had buried his pride to travel west with her.

Straightening the same dress she'd worn for four days, Dorothea adjusted her coat before rewrapping the wool scarf around her neck. The temperature continued to drop with each mile north.

A gust of wind pushed through the openings of the leather window covering, the frigid air causing a wave of shivers to pass through the passengers. Sitting back, Dorothea dropped her chin, dragging her wool scarf over her face.

She forced herself to focus on the destination and not the journey. In less than twenty-four hours, she'd join her daughter in Splendor and meet the man Francesca had chosen to marry. A man she had no intention of allowing her daughter to wed.

Kev Lathan positioned his rifle on the windowsill, guarding the trail from town. Vince had ridden within half a mile of the buildings, watching while not approaching.

Since his return, the brothers had taken turns standing watch for riders. It had been almost three days without anyone approaching. Days where they'd eaten, rested, and planned their next move.

The food in the root cellar would feed them through most of the winter. The stack of wood beside the house was dry, perfect for the fireplace and stoves. There were no pallets for sleeping or blankets, nor had the previous occupants left any plates or flatware for eating. What they had in their saddlebags would make up for the missing items. To men who'd been making do for years, the house was a palace.

Shifting in the chair he'd scooted to the window, Kev grinned at the sight of Vince snoring in the corner. His peaceful expression reminded him of when they were young, without the burdens facing them now.

He knew Christmas was approaching, suspecting it would be no different than what they'd experienced since losing their parents. Sparse supper with no presents. Not that they'd gotten much before the wagon accident. Their mother would sew each of them a new shirt, and their father would make a belt for both. If the farm had done well that year, they might even get a few coins to save or spend in town.

The memories were bittersweet. One minute, they'd make him smile. The next...well... He missed his parents and the farm so much his chest throbbed.

They'd done their share of robbing and thieving since losing the farm, but never killed or even shot anyone. Being charged with murdering a shopkeeper by an overzealous sheriff had ruined their plans for staying in Wyoming a while longer.

Since they'd been sleeping in a barn outside of Cheyenne when the man died, Kev knew the lawman had no proof. He also knew if they were found, the trial would be over in minutes, ending with their bodies hanging from the end of ropes. It was the way of many towns in the frontier.

They hoped to stay in the house through the winter, believing the chance of anyone showing an interest in the property during the cold season was remote. Even so, relaxing their guard couldn't happen.

That's why he and Vince had built an escape door in a downstairs bedroom off the kitchen, which exited out one side of the house. From the outside, it would be hard to detect. The exit might not keep a posse from following, but it would provide a few precious minutes to widen the distance between them.

Stretching his arms above his head, Vince closed his eyes on a wide yawn. "It's Friday, Kev. Why don't we head to town?"

Resting the rifle against the wall, Kev stood, stuffing his hands into his pockets. "What would we use for money?"

"I know we have some left."

"We're not spending the little we have on whiskey, Vince."

Crawling from the bedroll, Vince rubbed his face with both hands. "I want to ride in for Christmas Eve."

Stopping his jaw from dropping, Kev's expression changed from stern to incredulous. "Christmas Eve?"

"Yeah. The same as we used to with Ma and Pa. The church will be warm, and they'll have food. The women always bring food for after the services, right?"

Massaging his temple, Kev studied Vince, yearning clear on his face. Both missed their parents, the life they'd lost, but his younger brother experienced it more fiercely. How could he take this one request away from him?

"We can attend church on Christmas Eve. Afterward, we come right back here. No stopping at a saloon, Vince."

"Hell, Kev. They probably won't be open, anyway."

His gaze sweeping the room, Kev motioned toward their few belongings. "We take everything with us. We'll load the saddlebags with food before we go. I don't want someone walking in to see we've been staying here."

"No one's shown up so far."

"Doesn't mean they won't. We've got to be smart, Vince. If we return to find someone else here, we ride on."

"Sure, Kev. If that's what you believe is best."

Giving a curt nod, he grabbed his empty tin cup from the floor, stalking to the kitchen. The stove was still hot from the sticks of wood Kev had added. They didn't overload it, not wanting it to create so much smoke it would draw attention from any travelers riding by.

Filling his cup with coffee made hours before, he leaned against the counter, his gaze wandering around the room. The house reminded him of their family farm, and all the love their parents had put into making it a home. The same as Vince, Kev wished they could change the past.

Perhaps his brother's idea of attending Christmas Eve service wasn't as foolish as it first sounded. A few hours away, celebrating with others, might do them both a world of good. He just hoped they made it out of town without ending up in jail for a crime they didn't commit.

Enoch Weaver, who most considered Splendor's town drunk, sat outside the general store.

He'd found it to be a prime spot to watch the comings and goings of the townsfolk. Saturday morning had dawned with clear skies and a few degrees warmer than earlier in the week. It appeared Christmas Eve and the day after would be perfect for the celebrations planned.

"How are you doing, Enoch?"

He didn't have to look to recognize Hawke's voice. The deputy often joined him, sharing stories while watching the activities.

"Seems pretty quiet around town," Enoch observed, keeping his hands tucked into his pockets. A moment later, he shifted, pulling a flask from inside his coat, offering it to Hawke. Taking a swallow, he handed it back to Enoch.

"Compared to what went on over the last few months, the quiet is welcome."

"It certainly is." Sliding the flask away, Enoch nodded across the street. "I heard you discovered a boy in the Emporium. Related to those other two you already found. At least that's the story around town."

Bemused at how fast the story traveled, Hawke's mouth twisted into a wry grin. "I took him to the clinic. Joel needs rest and food, but should recover fine. Isabella Dixon is going to watch him, the same as Shep and Maisy. If there isn't a home for them in Splendor, we'll take them to the orphanage in Big Pine."

"Heard that, too."

Hawke shot a look at Enoch. "Is there anything you haven't heard?"

"Nope. People talk and I listen. The sheriff appreciates what I learn."

Stretching out his legs, he crossed them at the ankles, watching as a large wagon passed in front of them. "We all do."

"Are you going to escort Beauty to Christmas Eve service?"

Whipping his head toward Enoch, Hawke's eyes narrowed on him. "Where'd you hear something as foolish as that?"

Chuckling, Enoch pulled his hands from his pockets, clasping them in his lap. "You saying you'll be going to Zeke and Frannie's wedding alone?"

Shaking his head, Hawke hid a grin. "You're a crafty old man."

"I've been called worse."

Ignoring Enoch's question, Hawke's attention moved to the sound of the stage. "Might be escorting Beauty. Haven't decided," he lied. Ignoring their discussion on her taking in three children, he would be going with her to the church service and wedding.

Neither moved when the stage stopped down the street, the driver jumping to the ground. Opening the door, he helped an older woman to the ground. Catching her luggage the guard tossed down, the driver set it beside her on the boardwalk.

A moment passed before a man who appeared to be in his late twenties exited the stage. Hawke noticed he wore the same type of clothing as Francesca's friend from New York, Aaron Haas. Standing, he glanced down at Enoch.

"Suppose I should find out if the new arrivals need directions."

Touching the brim of his hat, Enoch's attention returned to the street. "Good luck, Deputy. My instincts are telling me you're going to need it."

Chapter Seven

Dorothea made a slow turn, taking in the main street, her nose crinkling. She knew Francesca lived in a rugged, frontier town. She hadn't expected it to be so insignificant. Turning at a shuffling sound behind her, Dorothea's brows shot up when the young man from the stage took hold of his luggage.

"Are you staying in Splendor?"

"For now," he answered.

"Then we should properly introduce ourselves. I'm Mrs. Dorothea O'Reilly of New York. As you may have heard on the stage, I'm here for my daughter's wedding."

Gaze wandering over her a moment longer than expected, he made a slight bow. "Mr. Elliott Endicott, from Boston."

"Boston? I have several friends in Boston. Perhaps you know them."

Huffing out an impatient breath, Endicott looked down at her. "Madam, I know many people in Boston. If you'll excuse me, I'm going to secure my room at the St. James Hotel." Bending to pick up his second piece of luggage, he walked past her, ignoring Dorothea's snort of surprise.

Staring after him, she failed to see another man approaching until he stopped a couple feet away. "Ma'am. I'm Deputy Hawke DeBell."

"Ah, Deputy. My name is Mrs. O'Reilly. I'm looking for my daughter, Francesca. Do you know her?"

The grin appearing on his face gave her the answer before he spoke. "Yes, ma'am. Will you be staying with Frannie?"

"She doesn't know I've arrived in town for her wedding. Is there a hotel you could recommend?"

Grabbing the luggage waiting by her feet, Hawke nodded at the other end of town. "I'll escort you to the St. James."

"I suppose it's the best you have."

Tamping down his amusement, he dipped his head. "Yes, ma'am."

Continuing down the boardwalk, he stopped for a moment in front of a building next to the bank. "This is Frannie's office. She's the only lawyer in Splendor, and we're real pleased to have her."

Dorothea stared at the embossed sign on the door. "The only lawyer, you say?"

"Yes, ma'am. She's searching for someone to join her."

Clearing her throat, she turned her attention to Hawke. "She's doing well then?"

"Most everyone uses her, including the largest landowners."

She fell silent as he led her across the street to the hotel. Entering, Dorothea's eyes widened. "This is quite nice." Taking a few minutes, she grinned at the number of beautiful wreaths.

"It's owned by two couples in town. One of them comes from a prominent family in New York with experience operating hotels."

"Deputy DeBell. How can I help you?" Thomas smiled at them from his position at the front desk.

"Afternoon, Thomas. This is Mrs. O'Reilly. She arrived on today's stage and needs a room."

"Of course."

Setting down her luggage, he tipped his hat at Dorothea. "Thomas will take good care of you. He can also direct you to Frannie's house."

"Thank you for your assistance, Deputy. I assume you'll be at my daughter's wedding."

"Yes, ma'am."

"So you know the man she's marrying?"

Hawke shifted to study her. "Zeke Boudreaux is a good man." He continued to consider her before turning away.

Watching him leave, Dorothea couldn't stop the sense Hawke had issued her a warning.

Elliott stood next to the window of his room at the St. James, his gaze wandering over the buildings housing a broad variety of businesses. Surprised at the activity on the street after expecting a sparse frontier town, he realized the reason for his visit might take longer than anticipated.

He didn't know where to start his search. The information provided by the private detective he'd hired in

Boston hadn't included the detail Elliott wanted. He'd learned his former fiancée had settled in Splendor, and come into a good deal of money, deciding to stay rather than return to the East Coast.

Two years had passed since his wife died. The loss never touched him, not the way losing the young woman he loved had when his father sent her away. Nellie Crawford had been the love of his life. They'd hidden their relationship for months from their parents. The poor Irish girl whose father owned a pub by the docks, and the wealthy boy born into one of the most prominent families in Boston.

The two young people knew their union was doomed from the first day they'd met outside his father's bank. Their hearts resisted the inevitable. Elliott found he couldn't stay away from her, his need so great it drove his actions from the moment he woke until falling asleep at night.

Shoving both hands in his pockets, Elliott recalled the day he'd realized his father had sent Nellie away. They'd raged at each other, a young man with dreams, his father with a future already planned for his son.

Realizing neither his father nor Nellie's would ever disclose her location, Elliott had eventually relented, marrying the woman his family preferred. Elliott's relationship with his father had never recovered.

Finding Nellie had become his first priority. Getting her back to Boston, his second.

"Taking care of three children is a huge responsibility, Beauty. Are you certain it's an obligation you're prepared to accept?" Francesca sat on the sofa in her living room, Zeke and Hawke across the room in two overstuffed chairs. She glanced at the men, Zeke's gaze assessing, Hawke's remote.

Clasping both hands together, Beauty lifted her chin, offering a serene expression. "I don't have to work and have no other responsibilities. Shep and Maisy both attend school, so it will be Joel and me most of the day. Noah has already agreed to add a third bedroom to a house on the next street, and Isabella has agreed to help when needed." She glanced at Hawke, uncomfortable with his obvious disapproval. Exhaling a deep breath, she focused back on Francesca.

"As an unmarried woman, I know it won't be easy to raise three children. I also understand there may be a husband and wife willing to adopt them, or someone else more suitable. If a couple expresses an interest, I won't object. Have you heard from Mrs. Paige?"

Francesca shook her head. "Not yet. Ruth plans to speak with people when they're in town for Christmas Eve services."

"And our wedding," Zeke added, grinning.

Francesca's smile matched his. "True. Ruth and I agreed to talk after Christmas. If I understand, Beauty, you're offering to take the children if no one else comes forward?"

"Yes." She lowered her voice to a whisper. "I don't want them going to an orphanage."

Hawke's expression remained impassive, even as his insides churned. Beauty hadn't asked, and he hadn't volunteered his opinion about her adopting the children. Family was a topic he refused to discuss. Not since the deaths of his wife and twin sons at the end of the Civil War.

"Nothing must be decided before Christmas. Let's wait to speak with Ruth Paige." Francesca offered an encouraging smile.

Unable to return the reassuring sentiment, Beauty stayed silent, sending furtive glances at Hawke. As always, he remained quiet. Hawke preferred people see him as rigid, a taciturn lawman with little patience and even less of a heart. Beauty knew the opposite was true. She also understood the relentless ache at losing his family. Her stomach twisted, wishing she'd never mentioned taking in the children.

Over the past few months, they'd become close friends, spending time together, sharing their pasts. His kisses had become more frequent, his desire to do more obvious. Not once had he mentioned courting her. She understood why. What decent man would want to court a woman who'd been another man's mistress? If she took in the children, there'd be no hope of a common future.

Before anyone else could speak, a firm knock on the door drew their attention. Zeke responded first, drawing the door open to find an older woman standing on the porch.

"Ma'am?"

"I'm looking for my daughter. Do you know Francesca O'Reilly?"

A gasp came from behind him. "Mother?"

Shoving past Zeke, Dorothea ignored the others. They met in the center of the living room, giving each other what he would describe as an obligatory hug, lacking any warmth.

"What are you doing in Splendor?"

Continuing to focus on her daughter, uncaring of what anyone thought, Dorothea removed her hat and gloves. Setting both on a table, she took a slow glance at the others. The men stood. Beauty stared, confused.

"Deputy DeBell."

"Ma'am. It's good to see you again."

Francesca crossed her arms, glaring at Hawke. "You know my mother?"

"He escorted me to the hotel after I arrived on the stagecoach. The St. James is quite nice."

"Mother, you didn't answer my question. Why are you here?"

Huffing out a frustrated breath, Dorothea pursed her lips. "To talk you out of going through with this farce of a wedding."

Hawke walked beside Beauty during the short distance from Francesca's house to hers. He didn't offer his arm, as she'd come to expect. What she didn't anticipate was the disappointment at the absence of such a normal gesture. Reaching her house, Hawke lingered outside when she hesitated to open the door.

"What do you think will happen with the wedding?" Beauty asked, not wanting him to leave.

A slow grin curved Hawke's mouth. "It will happen tomorrow evening as planned."

"But her mother?"

"Has no say in whether Frannie and Zeke marry. Dorothea may believe she has a right to press her opinion on them, but they aren't going to let her dictate what they do." Lifting a hand, Hawke swept a strand of hair from her face, dropping his arm when he realized what he'd done.

"You're going to attend the services, aren't you?"

Eyes crinkling at the corners, Hawke nodded. "I'm not missing Zeke losing his freedom."

"You don't truly believe those words, do you?"

"Might." The mirth faded from his expression as the light in his eyes dimmed. "Frannie's a good woman, and Zeke is devoted to her. Not much more you can ask."

Beauty glanced away, considering his words. "I believe they're a good match."

Removing his hat, Hawke fingered the brim. "Would you allow me to escort you to the church?"

The breath she'd been holding released. "That would be lovely, Hawke."

"Nellie? Is that you?"

Beauty froze, jaw dropping at a voice she hadn't heard in years.

Guiding her behind him, Hawke faced the man he'd seen getting off the stage with Dorothea. "What do you want with Beauty?"

Stopping, he ignored Hawke, looking at the woman behind him. "It *is* you, Nellie. I've been searching for you."

Grabbing Hawke's hand, she threaded her fingers through his. "Who are you?"

Walking closer, he rested his foot on the first step. "I'm certain you already know. It's been a long time."

When he lifted his leg to take the next step, Hawke held up his hand in warning. "Who are you?"

A smug grin tipped the corners of the man's mouth. "I'm Elliott Endicott. Nellie Crawford is my fiancée."

Chapter Eight

Hawke stiffened, hands dropping to form fists at his sides. *Fiancé*? He'd met Beauty almost a year ago, knew about her relationship with Kyle Forshew. Not once had she mentioned being betrothed to Kyle or any other man.

Beauty stepped around him, facing Elliott. "You're quite aware we are *not* engaged. The fact is, I haven't seen or heard from you since your father forced me to leave Boston years ago. If my recollection is accurate, you married within months of my boarding the train." Throughout her explanation, Beauty's voice remained calm, without emotion.

"My wife passed two years ago."

Her expression didn't change. "I'm truly sorry to hear that, Elliott. You must've loved her a great deal."

Rubbing his hand over his brows, he met her neutral gaze. "I *cared* about her."

Beauty gave a slow nod. "I see. Well, what brings you to Splendor?"

"I came for *you*, Nellie."

For the first time since Elliott arrived, her expression changed to one of disbelief. "I'm afraid you've made the trip for nothing."

Sneering at Hawke, his opinion of the deputy clear, Elliott shifted his attention back to Beauty. "Perhaps we could talk in private."

"Whatever you have to say may be said in front of Deputy DeBell. He's a very good friend, and knows a great deal about my life since leaving Boston."

"I traveled a long distance to ask you to marry me, Nellie. My father has passed, his estate is now mine. I'm in a position to provide you whatever you want. Has your deputy offered for your hand? Can he provide the type of life you deserve?"

She lifted her chin, not meeting Hawke's stare. "We are close friends, Elliott. You may not know, but I've also inherited a good deal of money. I don't need a man to provide for me."

"And marriage? Children? I know how much both meant to you." Elliott ignored the warning in Hawke's eyes, climbing the steps to stand before Beauty. "We can have the life we dreamed about, Nellie. I'm certain the deputy has been a loyal friend, but I'm in love with you. I want to marry you." Elliott speared Hawke with a pointed stare. "Is he willing to offer you the same?"

Even as his heart pounded in his chest, Hawke didn't respond. He cared a great deal about Beauty, valued their friendship. Did he love her? He wasn't certain. Not the way he did his late wife, Fiona.

What weighed on him most were the differences between the life he could offer Beauty, and what she'd have with Elliott. A small frontier town versus the world. He remembered Zeke struggling with the same. His friend had backed away from Francesca until coming to his senses. Hawke might not love her, but he had no intention of letting Beauty go so easily. Not until they had time to explore what was between them. He saw the instant anger on Beauty's face.

"Hawke and I haven't discussed marriage, Elliott. I can tell you he was there when my life was in danger. He didn't leave my side when I needed a friend. And he's never lied to me. Can you say the same to any of those?"

Panicked eyes met her unyielding ones before Elliott spoke. "How could I? Life was different in Boston."

Features softening, she reached out, taking his hands in hers. "My life in Splendor is much different than what you have in Boston. The challenges between the two can't be compared, Elliott. I don't know that I'd be able to return to a large city with the expectations of a family with your wealth. Don't forget, I'm the daughter of a pub owner and woman who cleaned houses to put food on the table. Your life back east is foreign to me."

"You'd adjust."

Dropping Elliott's hands, she leaned against Hawke's side, prompting him to place an arm across her shoulders. Besides on occasion slipping her arm through his, it was the most physical contact they'd shared. Even through his winter coat, his warmth seeped into her.

Beauty enjoyed his strength, didn't want to move out of his hold, knowing she had to. Straightening, she blew out a weary breath.

"Splendor is my home, Elliott." She glanced behind her. "I have a comfortable house and friends." Lifting her gaze to the man beside her, she took a chance. "And Hawke lives here. There's nothing else I need."

His hand settled on her lower back, although he remained silent.

"You need a man who loves you, who'll provide the family you've always wanted. I plan to stay in Splendor until you're convinced I'm that man."

Francesca poured an additional cup of coffee, her hand shaking with anger as she offered it to her mother. Joining Dorothea at the table, she forced a serene expression even as she seethed inside.

"You didn't have to send your young man away, Francesca. This decision concerns both of you."

"He's hardly a *young man*, Mother. And to be clear, he and I have made the decision regarding our future. You have no say in it."

"Of course I do. As does your father."

Ignoring the knots forming in her stomach, Francesca tried to concentrate on the final details of the wedding. Unfortunately, she, Zeke, and their friends had completed each item on the list, providing little to occupy her mind.

"It's unfortunate you believe your own daughter incapable of selecting a man she loves."

"Love." Dorothea bit out the word as if it were a curse. "People of our station marry for reasons other than love, Francesca. You know this is true."

"Which is why I no longer live with you and Father in New York."

"It matters little where you live. Your responsibility to your family remains. You're to marry a man of similar circumstance. One with the means to support you in comfort. An educated man, respected by those his equal. I doubt Zeke Boudreaux would fit at all in polite society, Francesca." Lifting her cup, Dorothea took a slow sip, satisfied she'd done her duty, while her daughter gaped in disbelief.

"Mother, are you listening to what's coming from your mouth?" Francesca continued before Dorothea could object. "Once I left New York, society's requirements no longer applied. They certainly don't in Splendor." Shoving from the table, she stood, dumping the lukewarm remains of her coffee in the sink.

"You're talking nonsense. Someday, you'll return home to take your place, as is expected."

Closing her eyes, she thought of Zeke, trying to imagine him in New York. A grin curved her mouth. There'd always been a mix of visitors to the large city. Still, a man such as him would be noticed anywhere.

"You're wrong, Mother. Zeke and I may return to visit you and Father, but I'll never resume the life I left behind." Sitting down, scooting the chair closer to Dorothea, she softened her voice. "Please understand. I love him. He's become a valued friend and confidante, a man I can rely on, someone who'd protect me, no matter the risk to himself. Do you know how rare such a relationship is?"

Dorothea remained silent for several minutes, a distant glint in her eyes. When almost five minutes passed without her mother speaking, Francesca reached across the table, touching her hand.

"Mother, are you all right?"

Blinking, Dorothea glanced around as if trying to recall where she was. When her gaze met Francesca's, her shoulders relaxed. "Is there more coffee?"

Taking the cup, she walked to the stove. "I should make a fresh pot."

"Whatever you have left will be fine."

Mouth twisting in uncertainty, Francesca tilted her head, studying Dorothea. Pouring what remained in the pot into the cup, she set it down in front of her mother.

"Thank you." Staring at the dark liquid, the older woman released several slow breaths before lifting her face, the normal uncompromising mask in place. "Would you and Zeke allow me to be your hostess for supper tonight?"

"It was a long journey, Mother. We should host you."

"Nonsense. If your father were here, he'd insist."

Chuckling, Francesca leaned back in her chair. "Only so he could control the conversation, Mother."

"True. Where shall we go?"

"The Eagle's Nest at the St. James is excellent. Afterward, we can escort you to your room."

"I'm not an invalid, Francesca. Still, it would be nice to be pampered and appreciated."

Her mother's words tickled a memory from when Francesca was young, living in New York. Dorothea had spent weeks planning the perfect soirée, meeting with decorators and caterers, delivering engraved invitations, and selecting exquisite floral arrangements.

When the event ended, her father climbed the stairs for bed, never acknowledging the extraordinary amount of work it took for such a successful party. She wondered if her mother was recalling the same. Out of respect, Francesca knew she'd never ask.

Redemption's Edge Ranch

"The weather's turning, Rachel. We should leave not long after sunup if you plan to help the women decorate the church." Dax Pelletier hung his hat and gunbelt on hooks, following his wife into the kitchen. Lifting a lid from a large pot, he inhaled. "Is this supper?"

"Rabbit stew. Billy and Shining Star brought them back after their ride this morning." Tossing the towel over her shoulder, she leaned against the counter. "They're getting close, Dax."

"They have to be if Billy's going to protect her."

Crinkling her nose, Rachel shook her head. "You know I'm not referring to Shining Star's protection. I believe the friendship is turning to something more."

"Running Bear is a clever man, sweetheart." Grabbing a cup, he filled it with coffee before joining her by the sink.

"You're joking."

"Not at all. There's a reason for everything he says and does. He's a shrewd old man."

"Do you mean he planned for them to, well...fall in love?"

Pursing his lips, Dax sipped the coffee, eyes narrowing. "Maybe not fall in love. I believe he hoped Billy would be so protective he'd at some point declare his intent to take care of Shining Star and her baby. Create a union of mutual benefit."

"Billy deserves more than a marriage of convenience, Dax. He's become an honorable, hardworking young man, who shouldn't be saddled with a woman and child he doesn't love."

Slipping an arm over her shoulders, he pulled Rachel close, kissing the top of her head. "Do you believe he cares nothing for her?"

Snuggling against him, she sighed. "No. I think he *is* falling in love with her, and possibly the baby. What if Running Bear returns to take them back to their village? Billy deserves more than to be shunted aside after keeping them safe."

"You're worrying about an event which may never occur. If Running Bear brought Shining Star here for Billy to take care of, I believe he intended much more than keeping her safe." Turning her to face him, he captured her mouth, deepening the kiss before raising his head. "I'm starving. I'll call everyone inside while you get supper on the table. Afterward, we'll get ready to celebrate our best Christmas ever."

Chapter Nine

Splendor

Hawke rested his arms on the bar, staring into his whiskey, ignoring the loud voices and laughter in the Dixie. He'd taken Beauty to the boardinghouse for an early supper, escorting her back home before stalking away, a sense of loss wrapping around him. An emptiness he hadn't experienced since the deaths of his wife and sons.

"How are you, Hawke?" Nick Barnett, one of the saloon owners, leaned against the bar, surveying the scene.

"Can't complain."

Chuckling, Nick motioned for his longtime bartender, Paul, to pour him a whiskey and another for Hawke.

"How's Newt?" Hawke thought of the last time he'd seen Nick's young son.

"Walking. Goes to sleep late and wakes up early." Nick took a sip of the whiskey, unable to suppress a grin. "I'm a lucky man, Hawke."

Tossing back the rest of the amber liquid in his first glass, he picked up the second, staring at it. Nick's comment about Newt speared Hawke through the chest.

Clearing his throat, he swallowed the rest of his whiskey, setting down the glass. "Yes, you are, Nick. Will you be bringing Newt to church tomorrow?"

"Sure will. Suzanne plans for us to sit in the back, in case he gets fussy. We'll be with Gabe, Lena, his father, and their children. You're welcome to join us."

Clasping Nick's shoulder, Hawke moved away, sweat forming on his brow. "Might do that. Thanks."

He couldn't get out of the Dixie fast enough. Sucking in gulps of air, he pressed a hand to his chest, his mind whirling with images of Fiona and his boys. Her long, reddish-brown hair, green eyes, and easy smile. His twin sons, with hair as black as their father's, running around their Georgia farm, laughing the way six-year-old boys did when causing trouble. The family he'd never see again.

Hawke hadn't experienced such an immediate, fierce reaction to memories of his family in a long time. There was the occasional devastating pang in his heart, the loneliness late at night, but not the breath-stealing jolt in his chest as happened tonight.

Straightening, he placed a hand on a post, supporting himself as he glanced around. Light snow created a dusting of white on the ground. He knew several old-timers were adamant the area was due for a big storm.

Across the street, a light in the jail drew his attention. Hawke couldn't remember who else was on duty besides himself. Since Hex married Christina, and with Zeke marrying Francesca, the number of single deputies had dwindled to him, Shane Banderas, and Dutch McFarlin. Gabe had assigned two deputies per night to make rounds in town. After Christmas, the sheriff had alerted everyone he'd rotate married deputies into night shifts until his budget allowed him to hire more people.

Crossing the street, Hawke thought of Elliott Endicott. The Boston dandy had made his intentions toward Beauty clear, promising to stay in Splendor until she agreed to return east.

The declaration had forced Hawke to consider his own feelings for the beautiful woman. They'd spent a great deal of time together over the last few months, especially since the threats on her life.

The two had enjoyed walks, rides, meals, and long, slow kisses. He yearned for more, wasn't ready to give her up. Hawke had begun to envision a future with Beauty.

It wasn't until today, when Elliott made his intentions clear, that Hawke understood he *did* want much more than friendship. Did that include marriage? He didn't know. What he could not consider were more children.

He thought of Travis Dixon. His friend had come home from the war to discover the same as Hawke. His wife and daughter lay cold in their graves. Travis had struggled with falling in love and marrying Isabella, demanding one stipulation. They would not have children.

The couple appeared to be happy, although everyone knew she hid the emptiness of not having a family by taking care of others. Hawke didn't want that for Beauty. She deserved a man who could offer her everything, including children.

Stopping outside the jail, he took another look around as he brushed snow from his coat, and stomped his boots on the boardwalk. Hawke noticed the empty bench where Enoch Weaver often sat, wondering what the older man was doing tonight. He needed to find him in the morning, make certain Enoch would be at the church service.

Entering the jail, he nodded at Shane, who huddled over a stack of papers. Lowering himself into a chair opposite him, Hawke reached across the desk to see what captured his friend's attention.

"Wanted posters?"

"Six new ones," Shane answered. "Gabe wants to make sure all the deputies study each of them." Holding up the picture of a woman with sagging jowls, he smirked. "Wanted for stealing from one of her customers." Setting it down, he held up another of a bone-thin man with a long beard and large ears. "Supposed to be the woman's accomplice. According to this, he was her bartender. They must not have stolen much with a bounty of a hundred dollars apiece."

"Where'd it happen?"

"Dodge City." Picking up two others, he held them out to Hawke. "Brothers wanted for killing a store owner in Colorado. Doubt they'd come this way. Hell, they don't look much older than fifteen."

Hawke studied the drawings of two young men with little more than patches of hair on their faces. "It's mighty easy to get a judge to approve one of these posters. Gotta wonder how many of them are accurate."

"Not our job, Hawke. We're to arrest them so they can stand trial."

"Would it bother you to learn we arrested someone who was railroaded by a jury made of angry people who didn't care about the facts?"

Shane leaned back in his chair, threading fingers behind his head. "Never thought about it."

Nodding, Hawke stretched out his legs, crossing them at the ankles. "Neither have I, until now. I'm curious is all. There's nothing we can do about it." Still, the images of the two young men stayed with him the rest of the night.

"Are you certain you won't allow me to pay for our suppers, Mrs. O'Reilly?" Zeke held Francesca's hand under the table, both waiting for Dorothea to give her opinion on their wedding.

"I invited the two of you, so I'll be taking care of the bill." Using her napkin, she touched the corners of her mouth before returning it to her lap. Signaling their server, she glanced between her daughter and Zeke. "Shall we order dessert?"

A few minutes later, with coffee and pie before them, Dorothea began the discussion the other two had dreaded. "So, Zeke. Tell me how you propose to support my daughter."

"Mother!" Francesca set down her fork, glaring at her.

"What? It's a valid question." Dorothea shifted toward Zeke. "Well?"

He sent a reassuring glance at Francesca before turning his attention on Dorothea, his voice firm yet gentle. "It's true I don't make a great deal of money as a deputy. I am frugal, saving a small amount each month to purchase acreage north of town."

"Where will you live?"

When Francesca opened her mouth to speak, Zeke held up a hand, stopping her.

"We plan to live in the two bedroom house I've had since coming to Splendor. My brother and niece lived there until he married. It's plenty big enough for Frannie and me."

"I want to see it."

"After we're married, Mother."

"Why not tomorrow?"

Francesca huffed out a sigh. "It's Christmas Eve. We'll be busy preparing the church for the service and our wedding. In fact, I'd appreciate your help."

Dorothea's face paled. "Me? What would I be doing?"

"There will be a good number of people meeting at eight in the morning. We'll be setting up food tables and decorating the community room, as well as the church. The reverend's wife, Ruth Paige, will be directing the work. She's wonderful, Mother. I believe you two will get along quite well."

"Who's watching the children, Frannie?" Zeke sent her a conspiratorial look, mouth twitching at the corners.

Biting her lower lip, her eyes sparked in amusement. "Of course. I hadn't thought of that. Mother, Zeke and I have been taking care of three orphaned children. Someone needs to watch them while we're working tomorrow. You would be the perfect person."

Eyes wide, her features twisted in what appeared to be terror. "Three of them? Absolutely not, Francesca. There must be someone with a great deal more patience than me. I'll help you at the church."

"Wonderful, Mother. I suppose we'll need to find someone else to watch the children." She sent a sly grin toward Zeke. They'd already made arrangements with Isabella to help them with Shep, Maisy, and Joel. Folding her napkin, Francesca placed it on the table before checking the time on her pendant watch.

"I have to meet Allie Coulter at her shop for the final fitting of my dress, Mother. Why don't you come with me?"

After a brief moment, when Francesca thought her mother would renew her objections to the marriage, Dorothea answered. "Of course I'll come with you."

Although it wasn't the enthusiastic response Francesca hoped for, at least she hadn't peppered Zeke with more questions. She knew it didn't mean her mother had given up on trying to dissuade her from marrying him.

Pulling out the chairs for both women, he brushed a kiss across Francesca's cheek. "I'll accompany you across the street to Allie's, then return to escort your mother to the hotel, and you home."

"It shouldn't take long. An hour at most." Sliding her arm through his, Francesca waited as her mother did the same. "Allie is married to another of the deputies, Mother.

Her business is quite successful. In fact, you'll find there are several vibrant businesses owned by women in Splendor. You'll meet many of them tomorrow."

Walking between the two women, Zeke thought of their wedding tomorrow and Dorothea's objections to their marriage. Her questions hit him hard, reminders of his own doubts about a life with Francesca.

It would be a couple years before he could finish purchasing the land from the Pelletiers. Then there'd be the costs of building a house, barn, and corrals. Weighing him most was the uncertainty of how much Dorothea's concerns would impact Francesca's commitment to their union. He wanted to believe her devotion ran as deep as his.

In twenty-four hours, his entire world would change. He hoped it would be for the better.

Chapter Ten

Redemption's Edge Ranch

Billy rested his arms on the top rail of the corral, observing several horses grazing. He'd been struggling with his duty to Shining Star and his desire to spend all his time working with Travis to ready the horses for sale.

Dax had been clear. His promise to Running Bear came first. Protecting Shining Star and her unborn child would take precedence over any other work.

Lifting his hat, Billy shredded fingers through his long hair, thinking about the real reason for his distress. *Shining Star.*

The young Blackfoot woman had captured his interest from their first meeting. They'd formed a friendship, of sorts, which was the reason her grandfather trusted him with her safety. At first, he'd been honored, welcomed the chance to spend time with her.

As the days and weeks crept by, they attempted to learn the other's language. Billy had learned the Crow language while a captive, but Blackfoot was new. He'd been surprised at her progress, and at the gentle way she guided him through hers.

What truly stunned him was her attitude about the pregnancy. Shining Star had shown no hatred toward the Crow warrior who'd taken her against her will. Even as the

Blackfoot people shunned her, and facing an uncertain future, she kept a serene countenance. He admired her...knew he was falling in love with her.

"Billy Zales."

Turning at her soft voice, he watched Shining Star walk toward him. Her splayed hands were resting on her expanding belly, a small smile focusing on him.

"Good evening, Shining Star. Are you feeling well?"

"Yes. And you?"

He nodded behind him. "Watching the horses."

Her gaze followed his. "It is a good time to be here. You will walk with me?"

"Of course."

It was the same almost every night. They would take short walks around the house or barn until Shining Start felt tired enough to sleep.

Tonight was different. For the first time, she threaded her fingers through his. The gesture surprised and pleased him. As they walked, Billy continued to be vigilant, his gaze sweeping the area ahead and around them.

Reaching out with her other hand, she captured several falling snowflakes. Watching them melt, she looked up, studying the darkened sky, brows furrowing.

"What is it, Shining Star?"

"This storm. It will not be easy, Billy Zales."

Glancing up, he saw the same clouds, felt the flakes drop onto his face. "A blizzard?"

Nose wrinkling, she repeated the word, brows drawing together.

"A blizzard is a bad storm," he explained.

Repeating the word several times, she nodded, satisfied she understood. "Yes. A blizzard."

A noise in the brush had him tugging her behind him. Dropping her hand, he drew his gun. "Stay here."

Taking a few steps forward, he whipped around at her scream. Coming at them were two Crow braves. One ran straight for Billy, knife raised, while the other grabbed Shining Star by an arm, hauling her to him.

Lifting the six-shooter, he aimed and fired, dropping one at his feet. Aiming again, his finger froze on the trigger when the Crow brave wrapped an arm around her waist, placing a knife to her throat.

Dragging her backward, gaze focused on Billy, the warrior didn't notice the men emerging from the bunkhouse, all holding guns.

"Let her go," one of the ranch hands shouted, moving with the others to surround him.

Struggling to hold onto Shining Star while looking around him, the brave's eyes widened in fear.

"Drop the knife," another yelled.

Removing his grip so she slumped to the ground, the Crow brave shot a defiant glare at those around him. Lifting his chin, he pointed at her.

"This woman is mine," he declared so all could hear.

Billy's stomach twisted. Was this the man who dishonored her? Keeping his gun in front of him, he stalked toward him.

"Shining Star is *not* yours. She belongs here."

Nostrils flaring, the brave's face reddened, pointing once more at her. "This woman with me."

"She's not leaving with you, son." Dax's voice broke across the tense group of men as he walked to Shining Star.

He carried no weapon, posed no threat to the brave. Kneeling beside her, Dax lifted her chin with his finger. "Are you all right?" The tears brimming in her eyes, the trembling of her lips, told him she wasn't. "Let's get you inside."

Billy bent down next to them. Scooping Shining Star into his arms, he ignored the Crow warrior as he carried her to the house and inside. Placing her on a bed Rachel indicated, he returned to join Dax.

Standing, Dax motioned to the dead Crow. "We'll load him on a horse. You'll take him home and never return. Do you understand me?"

Without being asked, Billy translated Dax's message into Crow.

Glaring, the warrior didn't answer, nor did he sheath his knife.

"Get your horses. No one will hurt you. But if you return, know we won't allow you to leave with Shining Star."

Again, Billy translated, seeing a spark in the man's eyes. "He understands, Dax."

"Let's hope he heeds my warning."

Tucking her arm through Zeke's, Francesca glanced over her shoulder at the St. James before leaning into him. "I don't know what to do about Mother. Question after question about us. She refuses to stop."

"Is she still against us marrying, or curious about me?"

"Definitely curious about you, and how you'll support our family. She refused to understand we'll both contribute."

Slowing, he came to a stop. "Both?"

Glancing up at him, she arched a brow. "Of course. I'm earning a decent living, Zeke. Between both of us, we'll do quite well." When he didn't answer or continue walking, she reached up to stroke his cheek. "Does the idea bother you?"

Jaw tight, he forced his irritation away. "Might."

Francesca understood it was a radical idea. Few men were open to their wives contributing to the family. Instead, they filled their time with children, church activities, and charitable events.

"It isn't any different than Suzanne running the boardinghouse, Lena managing the St. James, or Josie and Olivia owning the Emporium. All four are married and work."

Without responding, he continued toward her house.

"I understand Lena and Suzanne don't work as much since having their babies," she persisted.

"True." His steps didn't slow as he led her to the front door, throwing it open.

Frustrated, and more than a little concerned about his silence, she decided it best to let Zeke think about what she'd said. Pouring out the old coffee, she prepared a fresh pot, placing it on the stove. Facing him, she waited, stomach churning at what he might say. When he didn't speak, she took a seat in the living room.

His gaze wandering around the small space, Zeke sat down several feet away. "We need to talk about this, Frannie."

"You're right. I suppose we should've discussed it before now." The knot in her stomach, which began forming earlier, grew.

Leaning forward, he rested his arms on his thighs, clasping his hands together. "It's hard for me to accept you don't believe I can support you."

"I never said that."

"No, but you thought it. Your mother arriving, the questions she's asking, has made it clear we disagree on the responsibilities in our marriage."

Refusing to show her internal struggle, she forced calm into her voice. "You're right. Why don't you tell me your thoughts, Zeke, and I'll respond."

Meeting her gaze, he said nothing for several tense seconds. He couldn't miss the pain in her eyes, felt the tightening in his chest. Neither wanted to lose a shared future. Getting this straightened out now would be critical to their marriage.

"The same as most men, I plan to be the main provider. My wage will pay for the rent, food, clothing…" He rubbed the back of his neck, searching for the right words. "I hadn't thought about what you earn, Frannie."

Careful not to show her growing agitation, she gave a slow nod as an idea began to form. Smelling the coffee, she walked to the stove, pouring each of them a cup. She didn't notice the tense set of her shoulders, the way her hands shook.

Before she could turn around, strong arms came around her, Zeke's hands resting lightly over hers. The slight pressure had Francesca releasing the cups.

Pulling her against him, he placed soft kisses along her neck, his mouth resting at her ear. "Talk to me, Frannie. I need to know what you're thinking."

Turning her in his arms, he took her hand in his, guiding her back to the living room. This time, they sat next to each other on the sofa, neither releasing the other's hand. Sighing, she hesitated a moment.

"I understand why you intend to support our family, Zeke, and am all right with using your wage for necessities."

He quirked a brow. "But?"

"It's more of an idea."

"All right, sweetheart. Tell me your idea."

"I plan to keep practicing law, so there *will* be extra money." She bit her lower lip, continuing when Zeke squeezed her hand. "You've been paying on the land you're purchasing from the Pelletiers. I propose we use my wages to complete the purchase, then start saving to build a house."

Chapter Eleven

Francesca held her breath, sending up a prayer Zeke would see the logic of her idea. She also knew how hard what she asked would be for most men. Even for some women. Part of the issue was pride. Men were expected to bring in the money while women were to take care of the children and household.

She chastised herself for not considering her income a problem before now. Accepting Zeke back into her life, learning to trust him again, had been a huge step for her. The last issue she'd considered was the money from her profession.

"Zeke?"

"I'm settling it in my head, Frannie. This isn't easy for me. My father supported his family. Hex supports Chrissy and the girls."

"Your mother didn't work at a paying job and neither does Chrissy."

Lifting a hand, he nodded. "I know. Mother lived within the money Father gave her, and Chrissy does the same with Hex."

"Except Chrissy has a sizable inheritance."

She knew about the money from her father's estate, but Francesca and Zeke had never discussed her friend's wealth. They also hadn't talked about the money Isabella

Dixon, Caro Davis, or Abby Brandt brought to their marriages.

"Yes, she does."

"What about Isabella, Caro, and Abby? Their marriages are strong despite the fact those women are independently wealthy."

Zeke scrubbed a hand down his face before his gaze bored into hers. "I know about their money and the compromises they've all made to be together. I'll admit your idea might be a good solution."

"You do?"

He couldn't hold back a chuckle at the stunned expression on her face. Cupping her face in his hands, he grinned.

"I do. I'm not letting you go because of pride, Frannie." Seeing a tear escape to slide down her cheek, he swiped it away with his thumb. "We'll do it your way, sweetheart, and it's going to be all right." Leaning in, he kissed her, deepening it before pulling away. "There is one more issue we need to decide on."

Her grin froze. "What?"

"How are you going to keep your office open when we decide to have children?"

Brows rising, eyes wide, she drew away. "I forgot all about the good news."

"What good news?"

"The attorney who couldn't travel out here earlier is on his way now. In fact, I received a telegram a few days ago.

He expects to be here right after Christmas. There are a couple friends riding with him."

"And this is the answer to us having children?"

"Of course. He'll handle my clients until I can return to the office. "

Zeke's jaw ticked as he absorbed what Francesca was telling him. His voice was flat when he responded. "You plan to work after we have children?"

"I'd thought to. Are you against it?"

"Not unless you plan to have more than one child."

Pursing her lips, she stared down before lifting her gaze to his. "I was thinking three."

"Three, huh?" The corners of his mouth twitched even as his gaze remained impassive.

"Maybe four," she hedged.

"We'll need to build our house before number three, which means we'll be living out of town." Taking both of her hands in his, he pulled them toward him. "One child is a lot of work, Frannie. I know this because of helping Hex with my niece, Lucy. Two children, well..." He shrugged. "Unless you plan to hire a nanny."

"A nanny? My mother and father employed several for me over the years. However, they had their choice from many looking for work in New York." Pressing fingers to her temple, she gave a crisp shake of her head. "Actually, I don't want another woman raising our children, Zeke."

"That's good. I'd rather they learn from us." Kissing the knuckles of each hand, he let go, shoving up. "It's getting late." Assisting her to stand, he wrapped his arms around her.

Resting her head on his chest, she closed her eyes, allowing the warmth of his body to seep into her. "I'm not ready for you to leave."

Soft chuckles rippled through him. "Neither am I. We both know I have to, sweetheart. You'll be my wife by this time tomorrow, and there'll be no more nights apart."

Instead of heading to his house, Zeke decided a walk around town would help clear his head. The discussion with Francesca had gone well, yet agitation still plagued him. He should've thought about her money earlier, spoken with Hex and other men who had wives with independent means. Some inherited their wealth. Others worked, the same as Francesca, yet those marriages were strong.

Seeing the huddled figure on the bench near the jail, he sat down beside him. "Enoch."

"Zeke. Tomorrow's a big day for you and Frannie."

"Sure is. You plan to be there, don't you?"

"Thinking about it." Enoch covered his mouth, coughing several times before dropping his arm. "Darn body doesn't want to cooperate."

Zeke shifted toward the older man, concern etched on his face. "Have you gone to the clinic?"

"I'm not taking up the doc's time with this. They've got patients with real problems." Glancing away, he coughed again, this one more violent than the first.

Neither noticed Shane walk up until he spoke. "What's going on, Enoch?"

Instead of answering, the older man bent over at the waist, choking hard enough for Zeke to pat him on the back. "We need to get him to the clinic."

Rubbing the back of his neck, Shane shook his head. "Doubt either Doc Worthington or Doc McCord are there. May have to go to one of their houses."

Forcing himself to straighten, Enoch coughed again before pinning Zeke with a hard glare. "Don't wake up either doctor. There's nothing they can do for me."

"How do you know that?" Zeke asked. "Are you a doctor, as well as a lawyer?"

"Haven't been a lawyer for a long time, and I don't need to be a doctor to know I've got the consumption."

Lowering himself to his haunches, Shane waited until Enoch switched his gaze to him. "Not true, and I'm guessing you know it."

Closing his eyes, Enoch rested his head against the siding of the building, not responding.

Catching Shane's attention, Zeke gave him a conspiratorial nod before raising a hand. Using his fingers, he counted to three. The two slipped their arms under Enoch's back and legs, lifting him into the air. Trying to release arms now pressed against his sides, he struggled to break their hold.

"Put me down." Enoch's angry growl did nothing to change their minds.

"We're taking you to the clinic, then one of us will fetch a doctor," Zeke said.

"If you decide to go peaceful-like, you can walk. If not..." Shane shrugged, readjusting Enoch's weight when they stepped off the boardwalk to cross Palace Street.

"Fine. I'll walk."

Shane grinned at him as they set him on the ground. "You won't outrun us, Enoch."

Straightening his already rumpled coat and pants, he lifted a hand to his head. "Where's my hat?"

"Still on the bench," Zeke answered. "I'll go back for it once you're at the clinic."

"I'll get it now." Enoch began to turn back, stopping at Shane's grip on his arm. "Someone may take it."

"No one's going to steal your black derby," Zeke assured him. "Besides, everyone in town knows it belongs to you. Half the time, you forget it on the bench. It's not as if the townsfolk aren't used to it being left behind."

Mouth twisting in resignation, Enoch set his jaw. "I'll take your word for it, Deputy." Shoulders rigid, chin up, he marched past them toward the clinic.

"You think they can help him?" Shane walked behind Enoch, alongside Zeke.

"The doctor back home in New Orleans did a lot of reading on consumption. He had success using a technique some doctor in England tried. Found the treatment explained in one of his medical journals. Doc Worthington might know of it."

Reaching the clinic, Zeke couldn't stop himself from taking a brief glimpse at Francesca's house two buildings away. The kerosene lamps were still burning inside, tempting him to return. He'd left her place still a little uncertain as to their agreement on handling the money both earned, and what would change once they began having children. Zeke believed as long as they loved each other, there would be solutions to any and all obstacles.

Shane's voice pulled him from his confusing thoughts. "Do you want to wait outside with Enoch while I get the doctor?"

"You go ahead, Shane. How are you feeling, Enoch?" Zeke studied his face, concerned at the gray pallor of his friend's skin. "Do you want to sit down on one of the steps?"

"No, I don't want to sit down," Enoch bit out before the start of another coughing spasm.

"That doesn't sound too good, Enoch." Doctor Charles Worthington unlocked the clinic door, pushing it open. "I'll see you in the examination room on the right."

"I've got to get back to the jail, Zeke. Are you going to stay?"

Clasping Shane on the shoulder, he grinned. "I'm not leaving until Doc sees him. The rascal may try to make his escape."

"You let me know what Doc says. I've got a sense it's going to take a few of us to help the stubborn scalawag to do what he's told."

Waiting until Shane left, Zeke paced the waiting area, stopping every few minutes to watch the closed door to the examination room. Enoch, a man his fellow deputies had come to respect and count on to provide his opinions on the goings-on in town, was suffering from an illness hard to treat. If consumption did ail him, there might be little Doc Worthington could do. It didn't mean the doctor would give up. If anyone could find a cure, it was the man who'd opened a frontier clinic in the tiny town of Splendor when less than a thousand people had settled in the area.

Pacing to one of the front windows, Zeke's thoughts moved from Enoch's illness to the events of tomorrow. Any trepidation he felt didn't come from doubt about marrying Francesca. He loved her more than his life, and would do everything in his power to make her happy. His unease came from Dorothea O'Reilly's misgivings about him.

A sick feeling in Zeke's gut told him his future mother-in-law wasn't finished expressing her opposition.

Chapter Twelve

Beauty woke early, the night of sleep she hoped for never materializing. Thoughts of Hawke occupied her mind, including his obvious aversion to ever having more children.

They'd never spoken of marriage. Never admitted to loving the other. Beauty had accepted her feelings for the sometimes surly lawman, knew she'd marry him if asked. At least she'd been certain until his strong objection to children became clear.

Elliott seeking her out couldn't have occurred at a worse time. He offered her everything Hawke couldn't...or wouldn't. Marriage, children, a stable home. He'd said Beauty would have everything she ever wanted. She had no doubt it would be true. Did it include his love? Beauty couldn't help being skeptical.

Tossing aside the covers, she stood, making her way across the bedroom for her morning ablutions. Drawing her brush through long, white-blonde tresses, she came to several decisions.

First, no matter what Elliott had to offer, she no longer loved him. A large home with all the advantages of a life in Boston held no appeal.

Second, she would admit her feelings for Hawke. He'd either accept or reject her, but at least she'd no longer guess about his feelings.

Last, Beauty would quit her job at Ruby's Palace. On the last, she startled at pounding on her front door.

Slipping into a wrapper, she hurried into the living room, peeking out the front window. Hawke stood on the porch, his features drawn, lines of exhaustion creasing his face. Drawing the door open, she stood aside.

"Come inside before you freeze."

Entering, he turned to face her. "I know it's early."

Waving away the comment, she walked straight to the stove. "I'll stoke this and make us coffee."

His gaze wandering over her, Hawke suppressed a groan. Her nightdress and wrapper covered little of her gorgeous curves. "Why don't you dress and I'll make the coffee?"

Glancing down, she jolted at her almost transparent attire. Flushing, she turned away. "You're right. The coffee is in a tin next to the stove."

A slow smile curved his lips. "I know. Now, go ahead and change."

Heading to her bedroom, she stopped in the doorway, glancing back at him. "Why are you here so early, Hawke?"

The humor disappeared as his gaze met hers. "It's time we talk, Beauty."

Kev and Vince Lathan finished mucking the stalls where their horses spent their nights since temperatures began to drop several days earlier. Snow descended in slow, fat flakes, blanketing the ground while not stopping the horses from spending their days in the attached corral.

Whoever had abandoned the ranch put up a great deal of hay in the loft and ground level bins of the barn. Enough to get them through the winter. Between an excellent well and two streams close to the house, water was plentiful. The state of the buildings and property made them wonder why the previous owners had left.

The abundance of food in the root cellar would feed the young men for months. They'd hunted a couple days earlier, bringing back two rabbits and a deer. The cold weather would keep the meat fresh, eliminating the need to dry it for jerky.

Over the last few days, they'd cleaned the few pieces of furniture left behind, moving most of it downstairs to convert the house into a comfortable home. Surprising Kev, Vince had cut down a small pine, dragging it into the living room. There were no ribbons or other items to decorate it. Still, Kev appreciated his brother's efforts.

During one of their rides around the property, they'd discovered a small herd. About fifty head of cattle, all with the Diamond T brand, grazed less than half of a mile from the house.

They'd hitched Vince's horse to an almost unusable wagon and filled it with hay before heading out to the herd. Two trips had provided enough for a few days. After returning from Splendor, they'd haul out more.

Four wild horses were now in a corral on the opposite side of the barn. They hoped to find more in the hills around the ranch. For now, they'd found a place to hide.

"It's time we got ready for the ride to Splendor. Unless you've changed your mind, Vince."

"Give me ten minutes and I'll be ready."

Kev chuckled at his brother's boyish enthusiasm. All he'd talked about the last two days was the trip to Splendor for Christmas Eve. Kev couldn't help a small amount of excitement himself. They'd kept busy from sunup to sunset the last two days. The trip to town would give them a welcome respite.

True to his word, Vince mounted his horse ten minutes later, his brother following. Reining around, they rode from the barn, heading for a trail too narrow for a wagon. They'd spent considerable time deciding the best route to enter and leave Splendor without being spotted.

Not sure when the services would begin, they'd made the decision to arrive late morning. Being Sunday, stores would be closed. Not that it mattered. They had little money, perhaps enough for a whiskey apiece.

"Look." Kev pointed through the trees to a wagon on a trail about a quarter of a mile north. They were headed toward Splendor.

Pulling binoculars from his saddlebag, he made out a man and woman on the seat, plus three children in the back. One's arms were flailing wildly, as if telling a story. The others joined in, all appearing to talk at once. Even from this distance, he couldn't mistake their enthusiasm.

Vince twisted in his saddle. "Not far behind them is another wagon. Wait, two more wagons." Facing forward, a grin brightened his face. "The church is going to be plenty full. Which means there's going to be a lot of food afterward."

Kev's chest tightened at his brother's excitement as he strained to contain his own. He tried to be the rational brother, the one who made sure they had food, shelter, and stayed safe.

Riding into a town filled with Christmas revelers might appear stupid. Watching the wagons roll along, he found himself believing it would turn out to be the opposite.

Redemption's Edge

"Everyone ready?" Dax scanned the people who'd be heading to town. Most were in wagons, although he and several others chose to ride horses.

"We're still waiting for Lydia," Rachel called from her seat on the wagon.

Bull Mason's wife had baked until late into the night, making pies, breads, and dried fruit bars for the reception. Her contributions, as well as Rachel's, and those of the other women on the ranch, were safely packed in the back of the wagon. Even Shining Star had helped with preparing the food.

A moment later, Lydia rushed from the house she shared with her family, running to the wagon. "I'm ready." She climbed onto the wagon, joining Rachel and Luke Pelletier's wife, Ginny.

Dirk Master's wife, Rosemary, held the lines of another wagon. Next to her were Shining Star, and Billy Zales's sister, Margaret. Behind them, in the bed of the wagon, the younger children of the Pelletier ranch sat huddled together. In the center sat twenty-two year old Selina Rinehart, Lydia's sister. Everyone on the ranch adored her, especially the children.

Dax took another glance around him, confirming everyone was ready. Lifting his head upward, his lips pursed at the changing cloud formations. In his opinion, a blizzard was on the way.

Riding to another wagon, he relaxed a little, seeing it had been loaded with extra blankets, coats, hats, and gloves. Living a few miles from town, they always had to consider the chance of being stranded.

Seeing his brother, Luke, astride his horse at the back of the group, he lifted his chin before signaling for everyone to start moving. The increasing snow would slow their progress. If they didn't run into problems, such as a broken wagon wheel or lame horse, he estimated they'd reach Splendor an hour or two before noon.

Glancing behind him, the corners of Dax's mouth twitched. Riding not two feet from the wagon where Shining Star sat was Billy. He'd refused to leave her side since the appearance of the Crow brave. The night he'd showed with another warrior, the threat had become real to Billy and the others on the ranch.

Slapping the lines, Rosemary leaned toward the young Blackfoot woman, whose hands rested on her stomach. "Have you been inside a church before, Shining Star?"

As the question became clear, she shook her head. "No."

"There is a lot of singing and talking."

"Yes. Billy Zales has told me."

"There is going to be a wedding today."

Shining Star's brows drew together. "Wedding?"

"That's when a man and a woman marry."

Her eyes widened. "Yes. I understand."

They continued in silence as the snowstorm worsened. By the time they reached the school, located at the north end of town, they were brushing flakes from their coats. Dax and Luke reined to a stop at the jail while the rest continued down Frontier Street to the church.

The area around the church and community room was already filled with wagons and horses, indicating the large number of people who'd arrived early to help. Billy helped Shining Star to the ground, watching as she took in the sight.

She'd been to town one other time for an appointment at the clinic. Few people had seen her before they'd left town soon after the examination. Billy hoped there'd be no issues with a Blackfoot woman attending the Christmas Eve service.

Shining Star walked straight toward Rachel, lifting a pie from the back of the wagon. When everyone had something in their hands, she followed them into a large building behind the church.

Inside, men and boys set tables and chairs around the room while women and girls decorated the room with wreaths and strings of popcorn and berries. Ruth Paige directed those with food to place their dishes on various tables.

Unsure what to do next, Shining Star stood in a corner, watching as the room came to life. She'd never been to a celebration held inside such a huge lodge. Her family would have their gatherings outside, or smaller ones, of no more than a couple dozen, inside one of the larger tipis.

As she watched, Billy carried a ladder inside, leaning it against one of the walls. It was then she noticed hooks installed several feet above the ground. Bull Mason, Lydia's husband and one of the Pelletier foremen, strode inside a minute later, carrying a crate filled with lanterns. Setting it down, he filled each with kerosene.

Fascinated at all the activity, Shining Star failed to notice a small group of women in one corner, whispering among themselves. When their voices rose, she glanced behind her, surprised to see each of the women watching her.

Turning fully, she lifted her chin, not allowing the disgusted expressions on their faces to cower her. She recognized their intent. Shining Star had experienced similar shunning in her village when the women learned she carried a child. She suspected this group of women judged her in the same way.

"Shining Star."

Rachel's voice drew her attention toward the tables. Taking a last glance at the women, she made her way across the room to where Rachel stood with Ruth Paige. Recognizing the reverend's wife, a smile broke across her face. She'd met her more than once when she and her husband had joined the Pelletiers for Sunday supper.

Walking around the table, Ruth took both of Shining Star's hands in hers. "I'm so glad you're joining us today. This will be the first time my husband gives a Christmas Eve sermon, then presides over a wedding. I'm quite excited about Frannie and Zeke's marriage."

Shining Star glanced over her shoulder at the group of women, who continued to whisper while staring at her.

"Don't worry about them," Ruth said, letting go of Shining Star's hands. "They don't understand, but they'll do nothing to hurt you. You're fortunate the Pelletiers are protecting you. Few in Splendor would dare say anything against them."

A hand rested on Shining Star's shoulder, Billy followed the gazes of both women. "They should mind their own business."

Ruth's voice was quiet and firm. "Please don't worry about them. Either of you. There will always be people who refuse to understand those different from themselves. I will talk to them, as will Reverend Paige. I would advise keeping your distance from them."

"She'll be sitting in the church with me and others from the ranch. I'll stay with her afterward, Mrs. Paige."

"Excellent, Billy. Not that I believe anyone will do or say anything to threaten her."

Tired of them talking around her, Shining Star raised her chin. "They will not harm me."

Billy fought the urge to place an arm around her shoulders. Pulled from her village, shunned by women from the Blackfoot tribe, he couldn't help admiring her strength.

Rachel's voice caught their attention. "Shining Star, would you be able to help me bring in the rest of the food?"

Nodding, she left Ruth and Billy to follow Rachel outside. Stepping onto the stoop, she looked up to see storm clouds moving from the south. Shining Star shivered at the rapid drop in temperature. She'd told Billy a big storm would be coming soon. He'd called it a blizzard. Looking at the sky, she believed it a good word.

Joining Rachel, she reached into the back of the wagon to pick up a large square of canvas folded over several cloth-covered loaves of bread. Juggling them in her arms, she was surprised when a young man stepped beside her.

"Looks like you could use some help, ma'am." Taking the bundle from her, he nodded at the wagon. "Can you reach the last basket?"

"I've got it, Vince." Kev touched the brim of his hat at Shining Star before gripping the basket. "Where do you want these?"

Still staring at the two strangers, she shot a look at the door.

"Ma'am?" Vince asked.

"Oh, thank you, gentlemen." Rachel rushed toward them. "Please follow us inside." She motioned for Shining Star to go with her.

Stepping inside, Rachel walked to the first table. "You may set them down here." When the two men turned to leave, she stopped them. "I am Rachel Pelletier. This is Shining Star. I don't believe we've met."

"I'm Kev, and this is Vince, ma'am. We're just passing through."

"I hope you plan to stay for the Christmas Eve service. It will be quite wonderful. Afterward, you're invited to celebrate with us. There will be plenty of food."

"Perhaps we will, ma'am." Kev cast a look around as he answered. "Thank you for the invitation."

"The service will start at three o'clock." Allowing herself a longer look at each young man, Rachel turned toward the nearest table. Slicing two thick pieces of fruit bread, she handed one to each man. "Please take more with you into the church. This food is to share."

Watching her slip her arm through Shining Star's, they didn't respond before the two women moved to another table. Biting into the bread, Kev regarded his brother.

"I'm glad you pushed us to come here today, Vince. This may be the best decision we've made in a long time."

Chapter Thirteen

An unpleasant knot of anxiety settled in Beauty's stomach. She hadn't liked the stern look on Hawke's face, the way his back stiffened at his request to talk.

Shoulders slumping, Beauty wriggled into her nicest wool dress. Her movements were sluggish, not ready to hear Hawke no longer held an interest in her. A more depressing thought coursed through her. Maybe he'd never been attracted to her as more than a friend.

Reaching for a brush, she plaited her hair, flinging it over one shoulder as she stared at herself in the mirror. Eyes normally bright, with hope for a better future, were now flat. Her heart ached. She wasn't prepared for Hawke to walk out of her life.

Sucking in a slow breath, she let it out, forcing herself to stand on shaky legs. Selecting her favorite shawl, she draped it around her to calm the shivers. She knew they weren't from the cold, but what she suspected was about to come.

Meeting him in the kitchen, she grabbed two cups from a cupboard, filling each with coffee. A few feet away, Hawke stoked the stove in the living room. When he looked up, an unreadable expression met hers.

"Here." She held out the cup, taking a seat in one of the large chairs, Hawke taking the other. "What did you want to talk about?"

Taking a fortifying sip of coffee, he leaned forward, resting his arms on his thighs. "I care a great deal about you, Beauty. Have since soon after you arrived in Splendor." Taking another sip, he leaned back in the chair, his intense gaze locked on hers. "I want you in my life, and suspect you want the same."

Heart pounding in her chest, Beauty nodded. "I do."

Expression unchanged at her admission, his lips drew into a thin line. "If there's a chance for us to make a life together, we have some important decisions to make."

"All right."

"Might as well get it all out." Setting down his cup, he shifted closer, reaching out to take one of her hands in his. "I want to marry you, Beauty."

Releasing a relieved breath, a small smile appeared on her face. "I want the same."

Rubbing his thumb over the back of her hand, he pressed a kiss onto her cool skin. "But I don't want children."

Her heart thudded. The reality of his words slammed into her. Beauty knew they were coming, thought she'd been prepared to hear them. She hadn't. Children, a real family, had been her dream since falling in love with Elliott. Even as most dreams faded, she always held out hope for a loving marriage with a man who wanted children as much as her.

Throat thick, tears burning in the back of her eyes, she glanced away. "I see."

She hadn't moved fast enough for Hawke not to notice the misery on her face. He knew she'd wanted a family, children to fill a house and her days.

"What are you thinking, Beauty?"

Heart heavy, she forced herself to face him. No matter how much she loved Hawke, accepting his ultimatum would eventually lead to resentment.

She'd watched Isabella fight her burning need for children. Although her friend had said nothing, Beauty knew loving Travis wasn't enough for the kind, bighearted woman. Isabella ached for a family of her own, children with the man she cared so deeply about.

"I know you lost a great deal after the war. Your wife, sons, your farm. The tremendous pain has defined your actions, the future you see for yourself." Pulling her hand from his, she stood, pacing to a window. Staring out, she found her thoughts scattered. "I love you, Hawke, but I refuse to become a woman such as Isabella."

Brows drawing together, he stood. "What?"

"She's miserable, becoming more bitter each day."

"Isabella made an agreement with Travis."

"It was a devil's pact. Even so, she's determined to keep it, no matter the toll on her heart." Lips trembling, she forced the next words out. "I won't choose between you and the family I've always craved. It's unfair of you to ask me to."

Hawke glared at her, hands fisted at his sides, voice incredulous. "Unfair?"

Glaring back, she crossed her arms, refusing to back down. "What would you call it? I'm twenty-three, and you're asking me to forego a family for the rest of my life."

"You know why I feel this way."

Dropping her arms, she tampered down her anger. "I do, and I'm very sorry for the pain you've endured. The way I see it, if you and I decide to marry, we're starting over. A new life, with a second chance. Why shouldn't that chance include children?"

"Because it can't, Beauty." Shaking his head, he slid into his coat, grabbing his hat. "I'm sorry, but it just can't."

Heavy feet carried him to the door. A moment later, the front door closed behind him.

Body shaking, breaths coming in sharp gasps, Beauty stared at the spot where Hawke stood seconds before. Her feet were rooted in place, heart refusing to accept what had happened.

Seconds passed before she rushed to the door, throwing it open. Standing on the street, snow building on his hat and shoulders, Hawke didn't move. She watched as he lowered his head to stare at the ground. His chest heaved, shoulders shaking.

Without grabbing her coat, she walked outside, taking slow steps until she stood next to him. Sliding her hand in his, Beauty lifted it to her mouth, kissing each knuckle.

When she shifted to look at his face, her heart cracked. Tears streamed down his face.

"Come back inside, Hawke. Please."

When he didn't move, she slid her arms into his coat, wrapping them around his waist. Saying nothing more, she rested her head against his chest. It seemed forever, but may have been seconds, before he engulfed her in his strong arms.

Feeling his chest heave, her salty tears slid along her cheeks. Even with his warmth seeping into her, Beauty's body trembled at the icy wind whipping down the street. Without a word, Hawke removed her arms from around him, bending to lift Beauty into his arms.

Kicking the front door closed, he lowered himself onto the sofa, holding her in his lap. The silence stretched between them, Hawke rocking her in his arms, Beauty never wanting to let him go. Minutes passed before his fingers lifted her chin to meet his gaze. Without a word, his mouth captured hers.

Elliott Endicott adjusted his hat, smashing it down on his head before lifting the collar of his coat to help ward off the icy wind. Since he'd watched from his breakfast table in the Eagle's Nest, the storm had worsened, snow now at least a foot deep. The dark clouds appeared ominous. Their slow pace indicating the sky wouldn't clear soon.

Watching where he stepped, Elliott crossed the street, cutting between two buildings on his way to Beauty's house. He planned to escort her to lunch before accompanying her to church.

Careful not to slip on the steps, he hesitated on her porch to scan the street. From the time he'd left the hotel until reaching her front door, the volume of snow had doubled. He hoped the storm would pass by the time church ended.

Knocking on the door, he startled when Hawke answered. The two men stared at each other for several seconds before Beauty's voice drew their attention.

"Who is it, Hawke?"

Looking past him, Elliott saw the closed door to what he believed to be her bedroom. "What are you doing here?"

Cocking his head to the side, Hawke's lips twitched in amusement. "I could ask you the same."

"I hope you aren't taking advantage of Nellie," Elliott hissed, wanting to push past him.

"He is *not* taking advantage." Beauty marched from her bedroom, crossing her arms when she reached the men. "I wasn't expecting you."

Elliott didn't miss how she hadn't invited him inside. "I've come to escort you to lunch, then church."

"Oh. Well..." She glanced at Hawke. "You should've asked sooner. We already had an early lunch, as Ruth Paige invited me to join choir practice before the service. We're on our way there now."

Not giving up, Elliott ignored Hawke. "May I join you?"

"If you'd like, although I must warn you. The women will probably put you to work getting the church and community room ready for this afternoon." Slipping into her gloves, she missed his grimace, but not Hawke's snort. "What?"

"Nothing, Beauty. Are you ready?"

Picking up first one pie, then another, she handed them to the men. After putting on her coat and hat, she lifted a covered pot. "I'm ready now."

Setting down the pie, Hawke took the pot from her. "You carry the pie."

Over the few minutes Elliott had been at Beauty's, the storm had worsened. The wind whipped around them, fat flakes slapping into their faces, making it hard to see more than a few feet ahead. At one point, Elliott had to react quickly to avoid slipping on an icy patch.

Turning at the end of her street, all three hesitated at the sight of several dozen wagons, and even more horses, behind the community building.

"We should keep going if we want to make it inside." Hawke continued toward the buildings, shoving the door open for Beauty and Elliott to enter. Following, his gaze swept the room where at least twenty people still worked.

"Over here, Hawke."

Across the room, fellow deputy, Beth Evans, waved him over. "What do you have?"

"Beauty made roast with potatoes and carrots." He set the pot down, lifting the top.

"Oh, my. That smells wonderful. Leave it on this table, Hawke." Beth looked past him to the man standing next to Beauty. "Who is the man who came in with you?"

"Some dandy from Boston. They knew each other when she lived there."

"Don't like him?"

Pressing his lips together, he stared at the floor a moment before giving a quick shake of his head. "He wants to marry Beauty and take her back to Boston. So, no. I don't like him."

Eyes growing wide, she crossed her arms. "You aren't going to let her leave, are you?"

"Not while I'm still breathing."

"Excellent. I knew you'd come to your senses at some point."

Smirking, he shook his head, thinking of a few hours earlier. Their relationship had almost ended. Instead, they'd agreed to talk through their differences. It meant Hawke dealing with his past and agreeing to consider children. It would take a great deal of faith from both of them.

Beth leaned across the table. "You're a good man, deserving of happiness. If she'll make you happy, grab on with both hands and never let go."

Allie Coulter tacked up a stubborn section of Francesca's wedding dress, pleased with the result. "That should do it." Standing, she took a few steps away. "Much better."

"Yes, it is." Hex's wife, Christina Boudreaux, sat on the edge of Francesca's sofa. The same as Dorothea, the women had been tasked with checking for anything needing Allie's attention.

Dorothea tapped a finger against her lips. "It does seem a little loose around her waist."

"Since I won't be wearing a corset, I instructed Allie to sew it that way, Mother."

"No corset? I've never heard of a bride not wearing one under her wedding dress. It simply isn't done."

Casting an amused glance at Allie and Christina, Francesca whirled around, checking the dress again in the mirror. "Perhaps not in New York, but it's perfectly acceptable in Splendor."

"I don't even own a corset, Mrs. O'Reilly," Christina added.

"Josie Lucero and Olivia McCord sell beautiful ones at the Emporium, and I have a few in my shop." Allie rubbed her chin as she studied the tiniest details on the dress. "Seldom does one of my local customers request one. I believe you can change into the dress you'll be wearing for the church service, Frannie. I'll deliver the wedding dress and shoes to one of the back rooms of the church. Reverend Paige will announce an intermission before he begins the marriage ceremony. Have you already delivered what you need tonight to Zeke's house?"

A flush of heat crept up Francesca's neck and face at what she knew would be coming later today. "Yes. Zeke took over a satchel before going to the church to help the other men."

"We'll be taking care of Shep, Maisy, and Joel. Lucy and Cici are very excited about having them at our house for a couple nights." Christina stood, picking up empty coffee cups to refill them. "How else can Hex and I help you, Frannie?"

"You've done so much already. Plus, both of you are standing up for us. We couldn't ask any more from you."

"Helping you with the wedding and reception has been the most fun I've had in weeks. I'm so happy for you and Zeke. After today, I'll have another sister."

Stepping to Christina, Francesca drew her into a hug. "And you'll be my only sister. We're creating our own family."

Dorothea watched the interaction from her spot on the sofa. When leaving New York to stop Francesca from marrying a frontier lawman, she'd never considered her thoughts on the town and wedding might change. After getting to know Zeke, and the friends her daughter had made, Dorothea began to understand the new life Francesca had created hundreds of miles from her family.

Slipping out of her wedding dress and into the simple wool outfit she'd be wearing for the church service, Francesca took a seat next to her mother. They didn't speak, watching as Allie packed the dress.

"I'll meet you ladies in the back room after the church service. You don't need to bring anything, Frannie." Opening the front door, Allie hesitated. "Oh, no."

Rushing to look outside, Christina and Francesca let out gasps of surprise.

"Mother. Come look at this." The sky had darkened, prompting Francesca to grab a lantern. The light illuminated thick waves of snow cascading to the ground.

Rising, Dorothea smoothed hands down her skirt, closing the distance to the door with unhurried steps. "Goodness. It had slowed when Allie arrived."

As they stared, the wind shifted, whipping around to create funnels of snow. Allie set the dress down before returning to the open door. "It's good that most people have already arrived in town. It will give the storm time to move on before they go home."

Francesca didn't possess the same confidence it would pass through. She'd witnessed many storms in New York and during her brief time in Splendor. This one felt different. The clouds were darker, the wind stronger, the temperature carrying a deathly chill. At the thought, a gust of wind whipped through the open door and into the house.

"Close the door," Dorothea gasped, taking several steps away.

"Allie, please wait to see if the storm passes or lets up. I'm not comfortable with you going out alone," Francesca said.

"Frannie's right." Christina walked to the living room stove, tossing in more wood. "It's too dangerous to go out."

Allie shivered, wrapping both arms around her middle. "Perhaps it would be best for me to wait."

Francesca added wood to the stove in the kitchen, glancing out the window to see the storm had lessened. "Zeke and Hex will be coming to escort us to the church. We should all wait until they arrive."

"Cash knows I'm here. He'll probably come with them." Allie looked at her dress, frowning. "I had planned to change. This will have to do."

"You always look beautiful, Allie." Christina smiled at her friend. "What you're wearing is quite attractive."

"There's more coffee." Francesca held up the pot at the same time the front door opened.

"Whew!" Zeke stomped inside, followed by Hex and Cash. "It's nasty out there." Going straight to Francesca, he wrapped her in his arms. "The church is beautiful."

Hex removed his hat, setting it on a hook. "Isabella wanted us to tell you not to worry about the children. She and Travis have all five of them."

"Travis?" Francesca and Christina said at the same time.

Cash put an arm around Allie's shoulders, drawing her close. "Even if he doesn't want any of his own, Travis is real good with children. They're in the community building, playing with the other youngins."

"Is Reverend Paige still planning to start at three?" Christina asked.

"Haven't heard otherwise," Hex answered. "Gabe and Lena are saving seats for all of us. We should leave here soon. As bad as the storm is, the church is going to be full."

Helping Francesca with her coat and hat, Zeke leaned down to kiss her. "I love you, Frannie. Are you ready to spend your life with me, sweetheart?"

Smiling up at him, she stroked fingers along his cheek. "I've been ready for a long time."

Chapter Fourteen

Hawke entered the church, his gaze landing on Beauty within seconds. She stood on the other side of the room with Elliott by her side. They spoke with two deputies, Mack Mackey and Caleb Covington, along with their wives, Sylvia and May. Elliott appeared relaxed, laughing along with the others, while Beauty stood rigid beside him.

A fierce possessiveness gripped him. She didn't belong with the stodgy easterner who intended to take her back to Boston.

Hawke thought of Beth and her warning. *"If she'll make you happy, grab on with both hands and never let go."*

He never thought to love again. Not after the deaths of his wife and sons. His heart had been full when he left to fight for the Confederate cause. Returning, bitter with defeat, he'd found his farm pillaged, animals gone, and the family which meant more to him than his own life, dead.

Over the years, he'd hardened his heart, refusing to consider love after losing everyone. It hadn't been a difficult choice. No woman intrigued him enough to commit a second time. Not until meeting Beauty. She'd captured his interest from the start.

Her working and living in Ruby's Palace had never bothered him. He saw through her stiff façade as a bar girl serving drinks, to the woman inside. Brave and strong, with an inner pride few possessed, he'd spent months watching her from inside the dance hall. There'd never been an urgency to make a decision.

Much sooner than expected, he'd been forced to make a choice. Allow her former fiancé to steal Beauty away, or stake his claim. Hawke chose the latter.

Stalking across the room, he nodded to Mack and Caleb, ignored Elliott, slipping an arm around Beauty's waist. The gesture was clear to all three men.

Eyes wide, she began to sputter before he tugged her gently away from the others. "What are you doing?"

"What I should've done months ago." Walking to a corner at the back, he turned to face her. "Making certain every man for miles knows you belong to me."

"Well...I...."

"Are you denying it, Beauty?" His mouth twitched, already knowing the answer.

Brows drawing together, she studied his features, noting the longing in his eyes. "Not at all, Hawke. I'm yours and you're mine. Is that what you needed to hear?"

Brushing a kiss across her lips, he smiled. "I suppose it was." Glancing around, he noted the large, red bows, wreaths decorated with berries, and lanterns brightening the large room with a warm glow. *Christmas.* "Had you ever seriously considered leaving with Elliott?"

"No."

"No?"

"Did you honestly believe I'd leave all my friends, the life I've built, to return to a man who let me go without regret years ago? Did you believe I'd leave *you*?"

Rubbing his hands up and down her arms, he searched her face, voice lowering to a whisper. "I knew it was a decision you had to make for yourself."

Glancing past him to stare at a large wreath decorated with small white crosses, she let out a slow, shaky breath. Beauty hadn't dared dream they'd commit to a future together, and certainly not on Christmas Eve.

"Nellie. Are you ready to find a seat?" Lost in their own world, neither had heard nor seen Elliott join them. "The church is beginning to get crowded."

Not releasing her hands, Hawke turned to face the unwelcome intrusion. "We're not finished talking. Why don't you find a place for yourself. Beauty will be sitting with me and our friends."

Elliott's eyes flashed, fists clenching at his sides before he forced himself to relax. He took a step closer to Beauty. "Is that what you want?"

Her hesitation caused Hawke to squeeze her hands. "If you'll give us a few minutes, Elliot, I'm certain we can find room for you with our friends. Don't you think so, Hawke?"

Sighing, he gave a reluctant nod.

"Excellent. I'll wait over there while the two of you finish." Elliott smirked, indicating a spot several feet away.

When Hawke was certain they wouldn't be heard, he placed a hand on the small of her back, guiding Beauty to a small alcove. Cupping her face in his hands, he positioned them so no one would try to approach.

"We'll say nothing of our decision until after the wedding. Agreed?" Lowering his hands to her shoulders, Hawke waited.

Heart thudding inside her chest, Beauty took a moment to gather her thoughts. "And what decision is that?"

Hawke's brow lifted. "Getting married."

"I don't recall you asking me."

A grin tipped the corners of his mouth. Before he could respond, the sound of the church choir filled the large sanctuary.

"We should sit down, Hawke."

He wasn't ready to let her go yet. They needed to get this settled. "We aren't finished talking, Beauty."

It was her turn to smile. "I know."

Slipping her hand into his, she followed Hawke to where their friends sat near the front, then hurried to join those in the choir. Beauty didn't know where their next conversation would lead them, but the excitement streaming through her brought hope she'd not experienced in a long time.

"Please stand." Reverend Paige motioned with his hands, encouraging those attending to join the choir. A moment later, voices came together for *Joy to the World*, an old Christmas carol most learned as children.

When finished, the choir launched into *Hark! The Herald Angels Sing*, everyone's voices coming together in elation. Hawke watched Beauty at the front of the church, the joy on her face as she sang punched him in the gut. Around them stood their friends, Zeke and Francesca holding hands as they sang.

Beauty's gaze moved across the congregation, returning to Hawke over and over. She couldn't help wondering if sometime soon she and Hawke would be eagerly awaiting for their own marriage. After her forced departure from Boston, she'd never allowed herself to believe happiness with a man she loved was in her future.

For a brief time in Kansas City, she thought her benefactor, Kyle Forshew, might propose marriage. His betrayal had been one more disappointment. Finishing the second verse of the carol, her chest squeezed. What if Hawke's interest in her was temporary, one more journey into disillusionment? The thought sobered her.

When the song ended, Reverend Paige directed the choir members to join their families. Hawke threaded his fingers through Beauty's as they sat down, glad to have her close. Leaning toward her, he kept his voice to a whisper. "You look beautiful."

Shoving aside her concerns, she gave him a warm smile. "Thank you."

Reverend Paige's sermon focused on love, peace, and acceptance. At one point, he stopped, encouraging everyone to sing *Silent Night,* sharing the handwritten music passed around by the ushers. It was a new carol recently translated into English. Many in attendance joined in.

When the song ended, the reverend continued, finishing with an uplifting passage from the Old Testament.

The LORD bless thee, and keep thee:
The LORD make his face shine upon thee, and be gracious unto thee:
The LORD lift up his countenance upon thee, and give thee peace.

"For those of you who don't know, everyone is invited to stay for the wedding ceremony to join Ezekiel Boudreaux and Francesca O'Reilly. We will be taking a short break to prepare."

Several people stood, a few retiring to the rooms at the back of the church. Francesca, Christina, Allie, and Dorothea disappeared into a large room while Zeke and Hex walked into another.

The men emerged several minutes later, looking resplendent in white shirts, black pants, coats, and ties. They took a moment to meet with Reverend Paige before returning to the main chapel.

Not long afterward, Allie and Dorothea left the back, signaling the organist to begin playing a musical piece brought back from Europe by one of Splendor's citizens. Baron Ernst Wolfgang Klaussner insisted Francesca and Zeke include a magnificent piece composed almost thirty years earlier by fellow German, Felix Mendelssohn. After hearing the organist play the Wedding March, they'd agreed, grateful for the gift of beautiful music.

Holding Beauty's hand, Hawke felt a shiver run through her when Christina walked in, followed by Francesca. Not taking her gaze from her friend, Beauty leaned toward Hawke.

"She's stunning, don't you think?"

He nodded, although his attention remained locked on the woman beside him. "Yes, she is."

The ceremony didn't take long. When the door was opened for the short walk between the church and community building, a collective groan passed through the crowd. The storm hadn't diminished. Instead, it had grown into a blizzard, as bad as any the old-timers could remember.

Gabe, Noah Brandt, Cash, and Beau Davis secured ropes from one building to the other, leaving a couple feet between them. Everyone knew what to do. It took almost an hour for the entire crowd to move from the church to the large building for the reception.

Shane joined Hawke, a plate of food in his hand. "Did you see anyone leave?"

"You mean to go home?"

"Not a smart move, but with it being Christmas Eve, there might be some willing to brave the storm to get home. I'm hoping everyone stayed."

"With all the people moving from one building to another, I didn't notice." Hawke shot a look at Beauty, who stood at a food table, serving slices of ham and roast beef. Scooping up a forkful of potatoes, he chewed while casting sideways glances around the room.

"I didn't see Enoch," Shane said.

Hawke scanned the room once more. "He planned to stay at the clinic. Doc McCord is concerned about the consumption. He is encouraging Enoch to stay several more days. If the weather clears, I'll take him a plate of food."

"Do you see those boys standing in the corner with full plates?" Shane stared right at them, not worrying if they noticed.

Hawke followed his gaze before sending a knowing look at Shane. Both recognized them from the wanted posters. Unlike those images, they appeared to be young, lost...and scared.

"What should we do?"

A slight grin tipped the corners of Hawke's lips. "Go talk to them."

Chapter Fifteen

Gabe stood against one wall next to Cash and Beau, the three filling their stomachs with the feast the ladies had prepared. Swallowing a piece of roast, his attention focused on Hawke and Shane, who spoke with two cowboys across the room.

"Do you boys recognize who Shane and Hawke are talking to?"

Cash and Beau turned to see who Gabe referred to, shaking their heads. "Never seen them before, Gabe," Cash answered.

"Me either." Beau shoveled potatoes into his mouth, forgetting the cowboys talking with Shane and Hawke.

Gabe's brows drew together, worry creasing the lines around his mouth. "The blizzard is getting worse instead of better."

"Caro already made plans for us to stay at the St. James instead of riding home." Beau smiled as he talked about his wife. "I thought it was unnecessary. Now, I'm glad."

Gabe made a mental count of the people in the room. "I'm afraid there are going to be a lot of people stuck in town. We can put some up at the St. James, but most will have to bunk down in here or the church. I've already talked to Dax about the Pelletier people. If they couldn't make it home, he'd planned for them to sleep at Noah and Abby's house."

"That won't happen with the storm," Cash said. "Can't see three feet in front of you, which means they won't be able to get anywhere until this clears up. We'll have to stretch rope between the church and St. James for people to get that far."

Gabe lifted his hand, massaging the back of his neck. "What we need are blankets, buckets of fresh water, and access to the outhouses in back." Waving to his business partner, Nick Barnett, he motioned for him to join them.

Joining them, Nick didn't waste time with pleasantries. "This room and the church will have to be set up for everyone to bunk down, Gabe. We need to get to the hotel. The staff can gather blankets and food. Those who've lived here most of their lives, including my wife, are concerned the blizzard could last into tomorrow."

"Even if it lets up now, the trails will be too buried in snow to use tonight. Might not be usable for most of tomorrow," Beau said.

"If we can make it to the hotel, we can set up ropes to lead us down the boardwalk to the boardinghouse." Nick shot a look to his wife, who held their son while talking with Gabe's wife, Lena. "Suzanne has a storage room filled with blankets, and the root cellar is packed with canned goods. Between what's left in here, the hotel, and boardinghouse, there will be enough food for a few days."

Setting his empty tin plate in a stack of dirty dishes, Cash rubbed his hands together. "Guess we'd better get started."

Beau set his plate on top of Cash's. "I'll round up Shane, Hawke, Caleb, and Mack. That'll give us enough men to secure ropes between buildings and transfer supplies."

Within minutes, the deputies, plus Nick and Noah, worked together to plan a path between the church and hotel. Operating in teams, they braved the storm to collect ropes from the horses tethered out back.

Watching the activity, Kev and Vince Lathan grew restless. Their conversation with the deputies had gone well, the brothers answering some questions while deflecting others. They hadn't admitted where they were living or how long their stay near Splendor would last. It had been a relief when another man approached, explaining the sheriff wanted to speak with them.

It didn't take long for them to figure out what the men were planning. Vince turned toward his brother. "We should offer to help."

Kev rubbed a hand over his stubbled chin. He wanted to respond that the smart decision would be to keep to themselves, not draw more attention. The fact women and children huddled together to wait out the blizzard had him considering his brother's idea. Offering their help might prevent any suspicions the deputies might hold about them.

Pushing away from the wall, Kev motioned toward the deputies who'd returned with ropes in their hands. "Let's see what we can do."

Hawke lowered his head, dragging one foot in front of the other through the deep snow, making slow progress to the St. James. In one hand, he held an end of rope, the other securing his hat from pounding gusts of wind.

Shane followed a few feet behind Hawke, his hand wrapped around the same rope. Both were expert trackers with an unerring sense of direction. The other men remained at the church, feeding them more rope as they made their way across the expanse between the two buildings.

Reaching the hotel, Hawke wrapped an arm around a post, grabbing Shane's hand when he approached. Securing the ropes around two posts, Hawke tugged on each, feeling them go taut.

"Nick or Gabe should be coming across to talk with the workers in the hotel," Shane said. A few minutes passed before Nick followed the lines to the hotel. Behind him, Caleb, Mack, Cash, and Beau crossed the expanse carrying canvas sacks. They'd be filled with blankets and food for the people stuck inside the church and community building.

While the sacks were being filled, the deputies, joined by Kev, Vince, Noah, and Gabe, formed a human chain along the ropes to move supplies from the hotel to the church. Within minutes, the sacks were filled, provisions being passed to those who'd need them.

Beauty washed and cleaned plates alongside Christina in the kitchen area in back while May, Sylvia, and women from the Pelletier ranch dried them or placed towels across the leftover food. They knew it wouldn't be long before those milling about would return for more.

Lifting her head, Beauty smiled at the children sitting on the floor of the community room, playing quietly or listening to stories. The image caused her to think about the discussion with Hawke about a possible future together.

He'd yielded some, agreeing to discuss children while making no promises. Beauty loved him enough to accept the compromise. Elliott had arrived before Hawke proposed marriage, but the delay didn't bother her. She knew in her heart they had a future worth fighting for, and Beauty was prepared to fight.

The door to the main room opened, drawing her attention. Two young men she didn't recognize shoved their way inside, each holding canvas sacks bulging with supplies.

"Where do you want us to put these, ma'am? They're filled with food from the hotel."

Beauty shrugged, indicating an open space in an empty corner. "I don't believe we've met."

"Sorry, ma'am. I'm Kev, and this is my brother, Vince."

"I'm Nellie, but friends call me Beauty."

"A perfect name for you, ma'am."

"Thank you, Kev. Are you new to Splendor?"

"We'll be moving on once the storm passes. We're lucky we came upon the town when we did." Kev glanced at

Vince. "It was a nice service. We've never heard of a wedding on Christmas Eve."

"There's always a first time. Thank you for helping us. I hope you'll consider staying, and finding work in the area."

"Yes, ma'am. We just might do that." Kev turned to leave. "Come on, Vince. Let's see if there's anything else the men need us to do."

Heading straight to the side door, they drew back when Hawke and Shane entered with sacks loaded with blankets.

"Do you need more help?" Vince asked.

"It'll take several more trips to get everything over here. No sense all of us continuing to fight the blizzard." Hawke handed his sacks to Vince, motioning for Shane to do the same. "Why don't you and Kev distribute what we bring from the hotel?"

"We can do that, Deputy."

Hawke watched as Vince opened the sack, pulling out the blankets. He and Shane were certain these were the brothers on two wanted posters tucked away in the drawer of Gabe's desk. The same boys the two deputies had discussed without ever meeting them. Now that they had, Hawke was even more curious about the charges brought against them by a lawman in Colorado.

The way the two had volunteered to help people they didn't know impressed both him and Shane. He'd never met an outlaw who took the time to assist others. Now they had two of them, brothers who no more came across as killers as the Widow Cambridge, who died a few months earlier at the age of eighty-eight.

For now, the deputies would say nothing to Gabe. The blizzard posed a much greater danger to the town than the brothers who offered their help passing out blankets and food.

Hawke's attention shifted to Beauty. He needed to see her before going back out in the storm, but she wasn't in the crowded room.

"I'll be right back, Shane." Dashing off, he didn't notice the smirk on his friend's face.

Stopping to talk to townspeople and ranchers a few times, it took him a bit longer than expected to reach the kitchen. As expected, she was washing dishes, along with Christina and several other women.

The smile he received when she glanced up to see him lit his world. The speed at which she wiped her hands on a towel, and rushed toward him, assured Hawke his decision to marry Beauty was right. He still had to speak the words, leave no doubt about his feelings, and it had to happen soon.

Stopping inches away, Beauty reached up on tiptoes, placing a kiss on his chin. "You're frozen. Do you have time for coffee?"

"Wish I did, sweetheart, but we have to deliver the rest of the supplies from the hotel and boardinghouse. Keep several pots filled, as all the men are going to be ready for it soon." Ignoring the women staring at them, he cupped her face, bending down to kiss her lips.

"When people settle down to sleep, you're going to be right beside me." Releasing her face, the corners of his mouth lifted at the surprise on her face. After he left, Christina came over, followed by Isabella.

"Are you going to tell us what's going on between you and Hawke?" Christina asked.

Feeling a little lightheaded, Beauty continued to stare after him. "What?"

Snapping fingers in front of her face, Christina's mouth lifted into a grin. "You and Hawke. Is there something you want to share with us?"

Turning to face two of her closest friends in Splendor, her eyes lit with what could only be described as love. "I do believe Hawke DeBell may offer for my hand."

Chapter Sixteen

Transitioning supplies didn't take long, the blizzard letting up for a short period of time. As they'd brought in the last sacks of blankets, the blizzard's intensity increased.

Most of those stranded chose to stay in the community room due to the kitchen, proximity to outhouses, and extra stoves. Even Zeke and his new bride, Francesca, preferred being in the large area, not caring about it being their wedding night.

They'd carved out a small space on the floor, which would be shared with Hex, Christina, Cici, Lucy, and the three abandoned children. So far, a family hadn't been found to adopt Shep, Maisy, and Joel. It was becoming clear a trip to Big Pine might not be far off.

"I can't stand the thought of them being placed in an orphanage, Chrissy. With Cici and Lucy, Hex and I aren't ready to take them in."

"Beauty has talked about adopting them," Francesca said, as if it was the most natural solution.

"I know. She believes Hawke is going to ask her to marry him."

"I'm not surprised. It's been obvious how they feel about each other for months." Francesca glanced up to see Hawke and Beauty slowly walking toward them, blankets slung over their arms, stopping to speak with friends along the way. Lifting her hand, she waved them over.

"Marriage might change her mind, Frannie. It's hard as newlyweds to start with an instant family."

"I wish there was an easy answer. Zeke and I would adopt them, but..." She gave a small shrug. "We're still working out how we'll handle my job when we have children. I think he thought I'd quit."

"What ever happened to the lawyer from California?" Christina asked.

"He's on his way. Riding out with a couple friends. I thought he would've been here by now, but with the blizzard...who knows?"

"Is there room for us?" Hawke didn't plan to spend the night anywhere except next to Beauty.

"Plenty of space." Francesca indicated a small blank area beside her. "This should be enough for the two of you."

Spreading out their blankets, Hawke once again counted the number of people taking shelter with them. The count was the same as an hour earlier. He relaxed. No one had decided to brave the blizzard by venturing out on their own.

His gaze lingered on Kev and Vince, who sat several feet away. Each had a blanket wrapped securely around him, eyes wide open as if they didn't feel safe falling asleep.

Hawke knew Gabe and the other deputies had seen the stack of wanted posters received in the mail. None of them had matched the brothers with the images. Once the blizzard passed, he didn't believe it would be long before one of them put it all together. Hawke wanted their story before that happened.

Kneeling down to where Beauty sat next to Francesca, he took her hands in his. "I'll be back in a few minutes. I want to talk to a couple of men new to Splendor." He nodded over his shoulder, prompting her to look behind him.

"Are you talking about Kev and Vince?"

Brow rising, he glanced to the men and back at her. "You've met them?"

"They helped deliver supplies from the St. James. Kev said they were passing through."

"You know about as much as me. I'm going to see what else I can learn about them." Standing, he crossed the short distance in a few strides. "Mind if I join you for a spell?"

They shot anxious looks at each other before Kev nodded. "Not a lot of space, but you can take what's left."

"Won't be long. Just thought it might be a good time to learn more about you boys."

"Not much to learn, Deputy," Kev answered. "We're passing through."

"Hope you'll wait until the snow melts enough to follow a trail. It's pretty easy to get lost in these parts. I'm certain there are people who'd put you up a few days." Hawke wasn't certain at all, but hoped the comment would get one or both of them to talk.

"Might take you up on that." Kev adjusted his position, giving him access to his six-shooter. He'd never use it, especially in here with all the women and children. Still, the feel of it gave him a sense of comfort.

"Where'd you two grow up?"

"Missouri," Vince answered, regretting it at the look on Kev's face.

"Been through there a couple times."

"Where're you from, Deputy?" Vince asked.

"Georgia. Had a farm there once, but the war, and raiders, devastated it."

The brothers nodded.

"The war destroyed a lot of families. You talk to almost anyone here in Splendor and you'll find as many stories as people. Most are about starting over. You boys starting over?"

"Hope to," Kev answered.

Standing, Hawke settled his hands on his hips, looking down at them. "When the storm passes and Christmas is over, you two and I are going to talk."

Waiting until he'd left them alone, Vince's panicked gaze met his brother's. "What are we going to do, Kev?"

"I'm thinking on it. Could be he's curious."

"Could be it's more than that," Vince said. "Maybe he knows about the killing in Colorado. Might be there are wanted posters out on us."

"If he was sure we were on the run, he would've arrested us by now," Kev answered.

"Where would he put us? With the blizzard, he can't get us to the jail. Maybe we should get out of here, and ride back to the ranch."

"You've seen what's happening outside. Can't hardly see your hand in front of you. We wouldn't make it twenty yards before getting lost." Kev gave a quick shake of his head. "Best we stay here and talk to the deputy after the storm passes."

"What if he arrests us?" Vince's voice faltered, fear plain on his face.

Kev stared across the room where Hawke lowered himself next to the slender blonde woman they'd met in the kitchen. He wondered if she was important to the deputy, his question answered when Hawke kissed her cheek.

"If we run, he'll think we're guilty."

"They hang innocent men all the time, Kev."

"Yeah, but my instincts tell me that deputy might be our best chance of proving our innocence."

Dax Pelletier shoved open the back door of the church, taking the short walkway to the community building. Stepping inside, he stomped snow from his boots. The room quieted as he made his way around the families camped on the floor, not missing the wide eyes looking up at him for answers.

Stopping in the middle of the room, he made a slow turn, meeting their gazes. "There's extra room in the church for those who feel cramped. There aren't as many stoves, and you'd have to come through here to get food or use the outhouses, but there's more space. Only four families are using the church, so there's plenty of room for more. If any of you want to move, hold up your hands."

One hand went up right away, the man standing to face Dax. "I want the squaw and your boy to move over there. She don't belong with us Christian folk."

A few others mumbled their support, one other man standing. "I agree. She's pregnant, without a man. It's not right we should have to share space with her." His wife grabbed his coat, trying to get him to sit down. Swatting her hand away, he seemed to gain momentum. "Blackfoot, men or women, aren't welcome in Splendor. Don't know why you let her live at your ranch, Dax. No decent family would allow an Indian to mix with their women and children."

"I should go," Shining Star whispered, shifting to stand when Billy settled an arm over her shoulders.

"No. You belong here as much as anyone else."

Crossing his arms, Dax's jaw tightened. "Sorry you feel that way, Willard. As you and most everyone else here tonight knows, we don't turn anyone away who comes to Redemption's Edge for help. Shining Star is part of our family, for as long as she wants to stay."

"It ain't right to force the rest of us to bunk down near her," Willard continued.

Reverend Paige joined Dax in the middle of the room. "You're welcome to move your family to the church. I'll be happy to help while you carry your children."

Face flushed, the first man grumbled something incomprehensible before sitting back down. Willard continued to stand, searching the crowd for support. He shot an angry glare at Dax before focusing it on his wife.

"Get the children. We're moving."

142

She didn't move. "This room is better for us, what with the food and outhouses right out the back door. Besides, the youngest two are already asleep, Willard."

Grabbing her hand, he tugged her up. "I said we're going. Get the children ready."

"It's one night, Willard. We'll be going back to the ranch tomorrow," she pleaded.

"I've made my mind up," he snarled. Bending down, he lifted his sleeping boy into his arms. "Get the girl. We need to go."

Rubbing fingers over her forehead, she did as he said, attempting to grab the extra blankets while holding her daughter.

The room fell into a stunned silence. Most watched Willard stride to the door. Others kept their attention on his wife, their eyes filled with compassion.

"Let me help." Reverend Paige scooped up what was left on the floor. Following them to the door, he held it open. "This room will be open all night."

"Thank you, Reverend," she answered, her voice strained.

He offered a grim smile, closing the door behind them.

"Anyone else want to leave?" Dax asked.

When no one moved, he walked the short distance to where Shining Star leaned her back against the wall, Billy's arm still around her shoulders. Kneeling down, Dax studied her face.

"Most of the people don't have a problem with you being here. Don't let them bother you."

A slow nod indicated she understood. Leaning into Billy, Shining Star closed her eyes, hands splayed across her belly.

Standing, Dax walked to a nearby lantern hung from a hook, turning to face the room. "We'll be lowering the wicks for half the lanterns so everyone can sleep."

His brother, Luke, and Noah helped to lower the lights, giving a warm glow to the room. When finished, the men added wood to the stoves before joining their families. A welcome silence surrounded the large space as children settled down and adults prepared for sleep.

The blizzard could be heard through the silence, the wind whipping against the windows and doors. Instead of the storm's intensity diminishing, it had increased.

A loud crack, the unmistaken sound of a tree falling, had many of the adults sitting up to glance around. Not long afterward, a second crash had several men jumping up, rushing to the windows.

"Can't see enough to tell if there's damage," one said.

"Same with this side of the building," another added.

After a couple minutes, the men returned to their spots. Drawing covers over them, they were surprised again. This time, a lone voice, clear and strong, blanketed the room.

Beauty, standing alone, sang the new song introduced during the Christmas Eve service. *Silent Night* floated over a stunned audience.

At first, she continued alone. Then, one by one, other voices united with hers to form a beautiful chorus. They sang the first verse several times, the volume rising, peace filling the room.

When Beauty raised her hand, the voices slowed in unison, ending with the restful last lines.

Sleep in heavenly peace...Sleep in heavenly peace.

Chapter Seventeen

Hawke couldn't take his eyes off Beauty. He'd heard her hum while cooking, knew she could hold a tune. Tonight stunned him. In the pale light of the lanterns, the woman he loved looked and sang like an angel.

When the song ended, he held out his hand, helping her down beside him. "That was incredible, sweetheart." Her flush made him smile.

"My mother sang all the time. When I got older, we often sang together, trying to harmonize. It's been a long time since I've had an opportunity to sing again. After joining the choir tonight, and the conflict about Shining Star, singing Silent Night seemed right."

"It was perfect, and so were you." Regardless who might be looking, Hawke wanted to wrap his arms around her, kiss her until she couldn't breathe. After the performance, he refused to do anything to embarrass her.

Francesca rushed over, kneeling beside her. "You were wonderful, Beauty. And so brave to stand up there alone."

"It just happened."

"Be prepared. Ruth Paige is going to want you in the choir every Sunday." Patting her on the arm, Francesca slipped back toward Zeke, stopping to speak with May and Caleb.

A few feet away, Christina and Hex placed blankets over the children. Her sister, Cici, and Hex's daughter,

Lucy, were drifting off, as were Maisy and Joel. Shep sat cross-legged, his face grim.

Zeke moved from his spot several feet away to sit next to him, resisting the urge to place a hand on his shoulder. "Something bothering you?"

Shep's expression changed little except for a slight trembling of his lower lip. "No."

"Not sure I believe you, son."

"Don't call me that. I'm nobody's son."

The instant antagonism surprised Zeke. Shep had been prickly at times, protective of his sister and brother, but always distant when the conversation turned to his parents. He seemed to accept the fact the elder Waltons had left their children behind. Zeke and Francesca speculated Shep and his siblings were relieved to be rid of them. Tonight's outburst was unexpected...heartbreaking.

"Tell me what's on your mind. I'll do my best to help you fix it."

Shep swiped away a single tear rolling down his cheek. "There's no way to fix it. No way to fix anything."

"Every problem has a solution." This time, Zeke rested his hand on the boy's shoulder, surprised when he didn't shake it off.

Shep glanced behind him at his sleeping sister and brother, confirming they couldn't hear. A shaky breath blew through his trembling lips, his small frame quaking. Whatever bothered him wasn't insignificant.

"No one wants us, do they?"

Zeke's heart cracked at the pain in Shep's voice. What did one say to a boy who desperately wanted a family to adopt them? A child who wanted to be wanted.

"It's too soon to believe that, Shep. Ruth Paige hasn't had a chance to talk with many people. Neither Francesca nor I have given up hope."

Shep bit down on his lower lip, arms wrapping around his slender waist. He stared at the floor, his voice a whisper. "Why can't you adopt us?"

Zeke had expected the question, wished he had a better answer. He and Francesca had discussed adopting them, each time knowing it was too soon to accept such a huge responsibility. Neither were ready for children, baby or part grown. As the reality that no one might take them became clear, he knew Francesca would want to talk about it again. Both knew taking them to the orphanage in Big Pine wasn't a real option. Before he could respond to Shep's plea, Ruth rushed toward them, a man and woman following several feet behind her.

Reaching Zeke and Shep, Ruth held up her hand for the couple to hold up. "Zeke, do you and Francesca have a minute to speak with me?" She motioned with her hand to indicate the conversation would be private.

Squeezing Shep's shoulder, he stood. "Let's get Frannie and talk in the back."

A few minutes later, the three stood in the kitchen, the unfamiliar couple a few feet away appearing anxious. "What did you want to talk about, Ruth?" Francesca asked, casting a quick look at the man and woman.

"I may have found a family willing to adopt the three Walton children."

Francesca lowered her voice. "The couple over there?"

"Yes. Mr. and Mrs. Hugo Roland own a ranch south of Splendor. They've tried for years to have children, without success. Their house has enough bedrooms for each child to have one to themselves."

"I've never heard of them." Zeke cast a look toward them, noticing the apprehension on the woman's face.

"I'm not surprised. Heather is extremely quiet. They attend church, often sitting in the back, then leave right after the service. Hugo usually sends one of his ranch hands to town for supplies. Heather helps Hugo around the ranch, but they also have two hired men."

"They want all three?" Francesca felt a combination of relief and disappointment at the prospect of the children leaving.

"Yes. My husband and I have prayed with them several times about their desire for children. They see it as an answer to their prayers. Would you like to speak with them?"

Removing his coat, Hawke folded it for use as a pillow before propping his back against the wall and drawing Beauty to him. "Sit with me, sweetheart."

She didn't resist. The room had quieted, until the only sounds were the soft whispers of those still awake and the continuing storm.

Beauty settled a few inches away, needing to keep a small distance for propriety's sake. Hawke had no such concerns. Slipping an arm over her shoulders, he drew her against his side.

"We'll conserve heat by staying close."

Her hesitation lasted mere seconds before she relaxed against him. Tired, feeling better than she had in a long time, a small smile curved her mouth before lifting a hand to stifle a yawn.

"I'm more tired than I thought." She chuckled, releasing a sigh.

Hawke stroked her arm with his hand. "Are you too tired to talk?"

"No. Maybe. Is it important?"

"I'd say it is." Hawke kissed the top of her head.

Letting out a ragged breath, she straightened, looking into his eyes. "All right. What is it?"

"Are you certain waiting to make a firm decision about having children is something you want?"

"I understand your need to take more time, so yes, I can wait. You must know I'm praying your decision will be yes."

He stayed quiet for a moment. Over the last eight hours, Hawke had made his decision and couldn't wait to tell her.

"Listen to me carefully, sweetheart. What I have to say is important."

Rubbing her eyes, she felt a squeezing sensation in her stomach. What would she say if he told her he wouldn't change his mind about children?

"All right. I'm ready."

Sucking in a breath, he tightened his hold on her. Hawke had practiced the words over and over while moving supplies from the hotel. Revised them a little when she punched him in the gut with her singing of *Silent Night*. It was now time to share his decision.

"First, I love you, Beauty, and want to marry you."

Shoving up on her knees, her eyes grew wide as she stared at him. "Is this a proposal?"

"Yes, it is." Reaching out, he ran the back of his hand down her cheek. "Before you answer, there's another part to this."

Her hope plummeted. He was going to tell her he didn't want children. "Let's get this over with. Say it, Hawke."

His eyes narrowed a moment before a smile broke across his face. "I am willing to have children with you."

"What?" Beauty wasn't sure she heard him right.

"I'm asking you to marry me, and start a family." Holding his breath, he saw the instant it all came together in her mind.

"Yes!" Throwing her arms around his neck, she kissed him, not caring if anyone saw. "Yes...yes...yes."

All Hawke could do was hold her tight, and grin like a fool.

Even in the quiet of the night, news of Hugo and Heather Roland adopting Shep, Maisy, and Joel, and Hawke proposing to Beauty, spread as fast as the storm outside. Those who weren't asleep found their way to them, offering congratulations.

It was after midnight before the room quieted again so everyone could sleep. The children bunked down with the Rolands, while Beauty and Hawke cared nothing about appearances as they wrapped their arms around each other.

Francesca buried herself in Zeke's embrace, wishing they were in an actual bed in his house. This wasn't what she'd planned for their wedding night. Still, it would be memorable.

Wind whipped against the windows, the occasional crack of a falling tree waking some. Several times, a man or woman would walk to a window, checking on the blizzard. Each time, they returned to their spots with the same dour expressions.

Francesca didn't know when the pounding on the door started, or the current time. It continued, becoming more fierce and accompanied by shouts. Disengaging herself from Zeke's embrace, she rose on her elbows at the same time Gabe and Cash stalked to the door.

Pulling it open, they stepped aside as three men they didn't recognize crossed the threshold.

Without waiting for their hosts to ask, one of them brushed snow from his coat, and glanced around.

"I'm looking for Miss Francesca O'Reilly. My name's Griffen MacKenzie, and these are my friends, Bram and Thane MacLaren."

Epilogue

Three months later...

Francesca sat across the table in Griff's office on a Saturday morning, going through several files for the clients he'd be taking over. After arriving on Christmas Eve with two close friends from the Circle M in Conviction, California, they'd sat out the blizzard, the same as everyone else. They'd met many of Splendor's residents, found themselves impressed with what they learned.

The blizzard lasted through the night, passing through mid-morning the next day. Those who lived near town were able to ride home. The others were forced to stay another day, allowing some of the snow to melt.

While Griff became familiar with the town and Francesca's practice, the MacLarens were the guests of the Pelletiers. The ranchers had heard of and already respected each other—the largest spread in western Montana, and the premier ranch in northern California.

A few days later, Griff had accepted a partnership, while Bram and Thane had purchased an abandoned ranch east of Splendor, which came with a couple of squatters with enough experience to become their first two ranch hands. As much as they loved their family and Circle M, the MacLaren brothers had been ready to branch out on their own for the last three years, ever since their cousin, Cam, had married.

The surprise had come when Dax and Luke Pelletier proposed a partnership to supply horses to the Army. Their cattle business had expanded tremendously, as had their contracts to train and deliver horses. Their two trainers, Travis Dixon and Billy Zales, were overworked. Bram and Thane needed immediate work. The proposal provided a solution for both families.

"That's the last of them, Griff. The last three months working with you has been a true God send. The town and my clients respect you. The fact is, you've got much more experience than me."

"It's not always about length of experience, Frannie. Being able to get clients to hire you is as important. You've grown a sizable practice in a short amount of time. It's quite impressive."

Chuckling, she handed the stack of files to him and stood. "Helps when you're the only lawyer in town. It's time I get to the church for Hawke and Beauty's wedding. You're going, right?"

Shoving up, Griff grabbed his hat before strapping his gunbelt around his waist. "I'm meeting the MacLarens. I'd be honored to escort you there to meet Zeke."

Walking out the front door, Francesca couldn't help comparing today with Christmas Eve. The day was clear, a few white clouds dotting the sky. Nothing to compare with the blizzard of months earlier when she and Zeke married.

The ceremony proceeded with a full church. Beauty and Hawke made a magnificent couple, both dressed in their finest. Francesca wasn't sure she'd ever seen a more perfect couple. The taciturn lawman who suffered so much, and the former mistress of a Kansas City businessman. The broad smiles of those in attendance showed how little they cared about their pasts.

Afterward, everyone moved to the community room, where so many had spent a memorable Christmas Eve. Ruby had insisted her three musicians from the Palace provide music, while Ruth Paige's church women placed vast amounts of food on several tables. Across the room, five men stood together, all newcomers to Splendor.

"Griff, you remember Kev and Vince. The lads work for us." Bram motioned to the young men on the other side of his brother, Thane, his slight Scottish brogue setting him apart from the others in the room.

All those in the circle knew of the Lathan boys' background. How Gabe had worked with Hawke and Shane to clear their names. It had seemed a lost cause until a witness in Colorado had identified the man he saw murder the shop owner. No one was more pleased with justice served than Hawke.

"How is the partnership with the Pelletiers going?" Griff followed Bram's gaze toward a young woman standing with the Pelletiers. When Bram didn't answer, he snapped his fingers in front of his friend's face.

"What?"

"Who are you looking at?" Thane asked, turning to see the group across the room.

Bram shook his head. "No one," he lied.

Ever since his first visit to Redemption's Edge, his attention had been caught by a young woman with golden brown hair, bright green eyes, and a smattering of freckles. Selina Rinehart reminded Bram of several MacLaren women back home.

She could ride as well as most men, helped Travis and Billy with the horses, and her smile speared his heart every time she aimed it at him. Her nineteen made his twenty-five years seem ancient.

"That right?" Thane didn't hide a grin. "Isn't that Selina you're watching?"

Narrowing his gaze, Bram sent him a warning glare. "I'm needing food."

Amusement and knowing grins passed between Thane and Griff. Watching Selina join Bram at one of the food tables, Griff couldn't hold back a chuckle.

"Appears our move to Splendor is going to be real interesting, boys."

Holiday Roasted Chestnuts – Easier than you may think!

Ingredients

1 lb. fresh chestnuts, rinsed and dried

Directions

1. Preheat oven to 425°. Lay chestnut flat side down on a cutting board and use a serrated knife to cut an "x" about 1/3 of the way through the chestnut. Repeat until all chestnuts are scored.

2. Place chestnuts flat side down on a small baking sheet. Pour 2 cups cold water into another small rimmed baking sheet. Place chestnuts on top shelf of oven and baking sheet with water on the bottom shelf, directly below the chestnuts.

3. Bake until skin peels away from chestnuts, 20 to 25 minutes. Remove chestnuts from oven and cover with a clean kitchen towel. Let cool 5 minutes before peeling and eating!

   I love them warm and plain. For those who prefer a sweet touch, toss peeled chestnuts in melted butter, then sprinkle with nutmeg or cinnamon and sugar. Chestnuts will keep up to three days in an airtight container.

   Merry Christmas and Happy Holidays!

Thank you for taking the time to read A Very Splendor Christmas. If you enjoyed it, please consider telling your friends or posting a short review. Word of mouth is an author's best friend and much appreciated.

Watch for book eighteen in the Redemption Mountain series, *Paradise Point*.

If you want in on all the backstage action of my historical westerns, join my VIP Readers Group at
https://geni.us/VIPReadersGroup

Join my Newsletter to be notified of Pre-Orders and New Releases:
https://www.shirleendavies.com/

I care about quality, so if you find an error, please contact me via email at
shirleen@shirleendavies.com

About the Author

Shirleen Davies writes romance. She is the best-selling author of books in the romantic suspense, military romance, historical western romance, and contemporary western romance genres. Shirleen grew up in Southern California, attended Oregon State University, and has degrees from San Diego State University and the University of Maryland. Her passion is writing emotionally charged stories of flawed people who find redemption through love and acceptance. She lives with her husband in a beautiful town in northern Arizona.

I love to hear from my readers!

Send me an email: shirleen@shirleendavies.com
Visit my Website: https://www.shirleendavies.com/
Sign up to be notified of New Releases:
https://www.shirleendavies.com/
Follow me on Amazon:
http://www.amazon.com/author/shirleendavies
Follow me on BookBub:
https://www.bookbub.com/authors/shirleen-davies

Other ways to connect with me:

Facebook Author Page:
http://www.facebook.com/shirleendaviesauthor

Twitter: www.twitter.com/shirleendavies
Pinterest: http://pinterest.com/shirleendavies
Instagram:
https://www.instagram.com/shirleendavies_author/

Books by Shirleen Davies

Historical Western Romance Series

Redemption Mountain

Redemption's Edge, Book One
Wildfire Creek, Book Two
Sunrise Ridge, Book Three
Dixie Moon, Book Four
Survivor Pass, Book Five
Promise Trail, Book Six
Deep River, Book Seven
Courage Canyon, Book Eight
Forsaken Falls, Book Nine
Solitude Gorge, Book Ten
Rogue Rapids, Book Eleven
Angel Peak, Book Twelve
Restless Wind, Book Thirteen
Storm Summit, Book Fourteen
Mystery Mesa, Book Fifteen
Thunder Valley, Book Sixteen
A Very Splendor Christmas, Holiday Novella, Book Seventeen
Paradise Point, Book Eighteen, Coming Next in the Series!

MacLarens of Boundary Mountain

Colin's Quest, Book One,
Brodie's Gamble, Book Two
Quinn's Honor, Book Three

Sam's Legacy, Book Four
Heather's Choice, Book Five
Nate's Destiny, Book Six
Blaine's Wager, Book Seven
Fletcher's Pride, Book Eight
Bay's Desire, Book Nine
Cam's Hope, Book Ten

MacLarens of Fire Mountain

Tougher than the Rest, Book One
Faster than the Rest, Book Two
Harder than the Rest, Book Three
Stronger than the Rest, Book Four
Deadlier than the Rest, Book Five
Wilder than the Rest, Book Six

Romantic Suspense

Eternal Brethren, Military Romantic Suspense

Steadfast, Book One
Shattered, Book Two
Haunted, Book Three
Untamed, Book Four
Devoted, Book Five
Faithful, Book Six
Exposed, Book Seven
Undaunted, Book Eight
Resolute, Book Nine

Unspoken, Book Ten, Coming Next in the Series!

Peregrine Bay, Romantic Suspense

Reclaiming Love, Book One
Our Kind of Love, Book Two
Edge of Love, Book Three, Coming Next in the Series!

Contemporary Romance Series

MacLarens of Fire Mountain

Second Summer, Book One
Hard Landing, Book Two
One More Day, Book Three
All Your Nights, Book Four
Always Love You, Book Five
Hearts Don't Lie, Book Six
No Getting Over You, Book Seven
'Til the Sun Comes Up, Book Eight
Foolish Heart, Book Nine

Macklin's of Burnt River

Thorn's Journey
Del's Choice
Boone's Surrender

The best way to stay in touch is to subscribe to my newsletter. Go to
https://www.shirleendavies.com/ and subscribe in the box at the top of the right column that asks for your email. You'll be notified of new books before they are released, have chances to win great prizes, and receive other subscriber-only specials.